She wanted to be his wife more than anything, but it wouldn't be fair to him...

Emily had begun receiving emails from the Burlington Group, inquiring about her start-to-work date. They asked if she planned to take the summer off before starting to work full time. As much as she would have loved to spend the summer with Case, she nixed the idea. The sooner she began her job, the sooner her obligation would be satisfied and she could go home for good.

She started searching for an apartment online. She wanted to be close to the job but needed something cheap. A one-bedroom would be sufficient. No one would be staying with her, except Case when he came for a visit. She would try and fly back to Colorado every few months if she could afford it. She didn't want Case to pay for everything for her. She knew he would if she asked him, or even if she didn't, but she would remain adamant about that.

Case asked her to marry him, before she went back to Vermont, but Emily told him no.

"I want to wait until my commitment to the job is over," she told him. "Once I become your wife, my whole life will be dedicated to you, to you and me, and our children if we are so blessed but right now I can't make that promise. You deserve a full-time wife and I can't be that woman right now."

Theirs is an improbable story. She is a girl from Vermont, purposeful and dedicated to her calling in life. He is a rancher from the high country of Colorado who takes life one day at a time and never plans to be anything but what he is. When they fall in love, their lives change forever. She becomes his purpose and calling in life, and he becomes the only thing she really wants or needs. In the end, she is torn between the man she loves and the obligation she is honor-bound to fulfill—and whichever choice she makes is likely to break her heart...

KUDOS for *Magnolia Road*

In *Magnolia Road* by Jack Sprouse, Emily Quarters is a high school student with an autistic brother. Her parents want to send her brother Murphy to an institution, saying that they can't handle him, but Emily begs them to let her work with him and keep him at home. The parents will agree, providing the doctor agrees. Not only does the doctor agree, but he puts Emily down for a scholarship when she gets out of high school. When Emily graduates from high school, the doctor arranges for her to have a scholarship to the University of Colorado. There she meets Case MacNicol, an alpaca farmer. They fall in love, but Emily is obligated to go back home and teach for the group who paid for her education, and she will have to leave him for at least four years. Mixing a sweet romance and charming characters with a heartbreaking story of the working with autistic children, Sprouse shines a spotlight on a little-known but-all-too-common disability. An interesting and well-written book. Definitely a good read. ~ *Taylor Jones, The Review Team of Taylor Jones & Regan Murphy*

Magnolia Road by Jack Sprouse is the story of Emily Quarters, a young woman with an autistic brother, Murphy. Emily takes it upon herself to work with Murphy and teach him to read and write. Deciding that she wants to make autistic children her life's work, she wins a scholarship to the University Colorado, but there's a catch. After graduation, she has to return home to Vermont and work in the institute there for four years. She sees no problem with that until she meets Case MacNicol, who has an alpaca ranch outside of Boulder, Colorado. Now she is torn between her love for Case and the obligation she is honor-bound to fulfil. And if she leaves Colorado to go back and teach in Vermont, will Case wait for her for four long years? *Magnolia Road* is more than just a romance. It's a story of love and dedication, along with the consequences of making promises that you may not want to keep when the time comes, and the obligations you are honor-bound to fulfil may just break your heart—a thought-provoking and entertaining book. ~ *Regan Murphy, The Review Team of Taylor Jones & Regan Murphy*

ACKNOWLEDGMENTS

Thanks to my granddaughter, Cheyenne Middleton, for the wonderful cover art.

Thanks to Anna Grimmer Tidwell and Nicole Cagle Grimmer, teachers of autistic students who provided information on the subject.

Thanks to Kai Sensabaugh, my seven-year-old grandson for information on the *Angry Birds* game

And finally, thanks to Bob Amos and the group, Front Range, for permission to use the lyrics to the song, "High Mountain Meadow," written by Bob Amos, Stark Brook Music, BMI. It's one of my favorite songs.

MAGNOLIA ROAD

Jack Sprouse

A Black Opal Books Publication

GENRE: CONTEMPORARY ROMANCE/WOMEN'S FICTION

MAGNOLIA ROAD
Copyright © 2016 by Jack Sprouse
Cover Design by Cheyenne Middleton
All cover art copyright © 2017
All Rights Reserved
Lyrics to "High Mountain Meadow" used with permission
Print ISBN: 978-1-626947-87-0

First Publication: NOVEMBER 2017

Published by Black Opal Books **http://www.blackopalbooks.com**

DEDICATION

This book is dedicated to Bill Starr,
my best Colorado friend for thirty-five years

Table of Contents

CHAPTER 1

Emily

The quiet scenic town of Middlebury, in Addison County, Vermont, lay in the central western part of the Green Mountain State. It was an almost idyllic village of picturesque buildings and surrounding countryside that evokes sentient emotions and love of the natural wonder of God's creation. The town was cut in half by the intrusion of Otter Creek, which ran through it and served to enhance the already unique personality of the little town.

The Quarters family, Norman and Edna and their two children Emily and Murphy, owned a house on South Street on the west side of the creek. An old style two-story home with a walk-around porch that circumvented the entire house made it a comfortable and pleasant place in which to live and grow up.

Emily, the oldest child, was gifted from birth and excelled at everything she did. She maintained honor roll grade point averages all through her lower grades and entered Middlebury Union High School with a solid 4.0 GPA. Her life might have held greater promise for her, except for an unfortunate set of circumstances that had afflicted her family.

Her younger brother Murphy, five years her junior, had been born with Autism. It did not become immediately noticeable until the boy was about three years old and he didn't start talking until he was five. The family was thrown into turmoil over the revelation that their son and brother was a special-needs child.

By the time he was nine, they were almost distraught.

"What are we going to do, Norman?" Edna Quarters wailed at her husband. "You know we can't afford to take care of a retarded kid."

"Murphy is not retarded, Mother," her daughter, Emily, shot back, "I think he's autistic."

"What is autistic, Emily?" her father asked.

"I don't know everything about it but he's not retarded. He may be slow at learning, but he is also very bright. He draws things and he talks to me, not well, but I'm trying to help him speak more clearly."

"But they know so much more about taking care of

those kinds of problems at state facilities than you can ever know," Norman said. "Your mother and I are too old to deal with this."

"I've been studying it on the internet, and I've learned a lot, Dad. He speaks when we're alone. He just doesn't talk when he's around other people. He gets scared when he's around people."

"We've talked to the doctors from the local hospital, Emily. They think it would be best if we send him to Burlington. They can take care of him there, and he can be taught by professionals."

"But they're not family. Let me talk to them and show them what I've done with him, and maybe I can convince them that it's better if he stays with us."

They met at the local hospital facility, and Emily took Murphy with her. She had him read from a couple of children's books she had used to teach him. "I don't believe his unclear speaking is physical," she told the doctors. "He doesn't have a cleft palette or anything else that I can see. I think it's all mental related. He just doesn't form his words properly."

"So, can you show us what you do, Emily?" Doctor Gregory asked her.

"Sure, Doctor. Murphy, come over here, please. Remember the name of your favorite stuffed bear?"

Murphy shook his head.

"Oh, come on, Murph. You remember, Jerome Bear, don't you?"

"Jome Bear," the boy said.

"No, now watch my mouth, Murph."

The boy turned his head and looked at her mouth.

"Say Juh."

"Juh," he said.

"Rome, Juh rome."

He repeated the phrase, "Juh Rome. Juhrome."

"Now say Jerome Bear."

And he repeated it.

She gave them several more examples and Murphy followed her lead just as he did at home with her.

"So, what do you plan to do about Murphy once you graduate from high school, Emily? You're not going to stay home and devote your life to teaching him, are you?"

"No, Doctor, I suppose when that time comes I'll have to let my parents decide what is best for my little brother."

"Do you plan to go to college? And if so what field do you plan to go into?"

"I'd like to teach special needs children, Doctor."

"I kind of figured that might be where you were headed. I'd encourage you to stick with that. You have an aptitude for it, I think."

"Thank you, sir," she said. "I taught his him to draw by using tracing paper at first but eventually he learned to look at objects and draw them without having to trace them."

"I see," Doctor Gregory said. "Well, I'd have to say

you've done a pretty good job for a girl with no formal training."

After Emily left his office, Doctor Gregory picked up the phone and dialed a number in Burlington. "I'd like to speak to Doctor Shelby," he said.

"May I say who is calling, please?" the reception said.

"This is Allen Gregory in Middlebury."

"Hold, please."

"Allen, this is Jason Shelby, how are you?"

"Just fine, Jason. It's been a long time, hasn't it?"

"Indeed, it has," Shelby replied. "What's on your mind?"

"There's a young lady here in Middlebury who has been teaching her little brother how to communicate, write, and draw, and will, no doubt be teaching him to read and write before she is finished with him. He's autistic. The parents wanted to send him to you guys but the daughter begged them to keep him at home so she could work with him."

"Really? She sounds like somebody we might want to talk to. How old is this young lady, Allen?"

"She's fourteen and has a very high GPA, and that's what I was thinking too, Jason. Why don't I email you her information, and you do with it what you think is best?"

"Thanks, Allen, I'll certainly check her out. Thank you. We're not ready at this time for another project but as soon as we are, I'll contact the girl"

"She's a very engaging girl and as smart as they come."

Emily was fiercely protective of Murphy. When some rude person would make fun of him, he would immediately incur the wrath of Murphy's older sister. She never held back when chastising someone for their stupidity. A boy in high school once asked her: "Hey, Emily, where's Arnie?

"Who is Arnie, Jimmy?"

"Arnie Grape, the retard, your brother."

"He's not a retard, you stupid ass," she screamed at the boy who had overstepped his boundaries. "He's smarter than you are."

The boy, seeing her anger, made a feeble attempt to apologize but Emily would not hear it. She brushed him off and never spoke to him again. Her fellow students soon learned what an ill-advised act of inconsideration it was to cross Emily Quarters when the subject was her brother Murphy.

At sixteen, Emily had started to blossom. She didn't think of herself as overly attractive and she dressed down to detract from her rapidly developing perfect figure and abundant breasts. She refrained from wearing tight pants and, instead, wore baggy sweaters and skirts with legwarmers, which served two purposes. They kept her legs warm in the cold Vermont winters, and they took attention away from her shapely legs.

None of her efforts, however, managed to fool or discourage Danny Miller. Danny took a liking to Emily and, even had she worn a sleeping bag to school, he would still have been smitten. Nothing Emily did could ease his pain. Danny was nothing, if not persuasive, and Emily eventually consented to a going to a movie with him.

"There's a party at Jimmy Snowden's house on Saturday, Emily, will you go with me?"

"Drunk jocks are not really my thing, Danny," she told him.

"But you'll be with me," he said, "nobody will mess with you."

"Okay. As long as you promise not to get drunk."

"I promise," he said, and he kept his promise, sort of. He didn't get really drunk. "I wish you would brush your hair so that it stays out of your face," he said as he pulled his car into the park.

"Why? she asked.

"Because you're beautiful, Emily."

"I don't think I'm beautiful, Danny."

"I do. You are beautiful." He took her hand and pulled her across the seat to him, put his arm around her, and stated kissing her. She didn't resist.

"I love you, Emily," he told her, in between kisses.

"I'm not ready to fall in love, Danny. I have a lot of plans for after high school."

"I know you do, and I won't interfere with them. I

just want to be a part of you. Will you be my girl?"

"I suppose, Danny, but you know I spend a lot of time working with my brother. I don't have a lot of free time. And I plan to go to college to get a teaching degree. I don't really fit into the crowd you run in."

"You don't have to, Emily. We can date on the weekend, go to a movie, or out to eat, or something like that. I just want to be a part of 'your' crowd."

"All right, that sounds okay," she told him, "that's actually very sweet."

He started kissing her again and she felt herself getting aroused.

"Okay, that's enough, Danny, this could go too far."

He never got angry about it when she backed off, and he was always apologetic. When she gave it some thought, she realized that Danny actually was very nice to her. She just wasn't sure at that time that she wanted the kind of serious relationship with him that he wanted with her.

"I love you, Emily," he always said when he dropped her off at her house, but she never responded in kind. She wasn't entirely convinced that she would ever fall in love with Danny Miller, or anyone else.

Well-made plans, however, rarely survive contact with human emotions, and Emily—as disciplined and as driven as she was—was, after all, just a girl. And girls had feelings, and hormones, and when male and female bodies touch each other, intellect and reason often lose their influence.

Danny drove to the park again on Saturday night, parked in a secluded area, and began kissing Emily. "I love your lips, Emily. I get dizzy when I kiss you."

She started chuckling at his seriousness. "You've been watching too many movies, Danny."

"I'm serious, Emily. Something happens inside me when I kiss you. It just feels good," he said. "You must feel it too because you kiss me back."

"I enjoy kissing you but sometimes kissing can lead to going too far and the consequences of that can outweigh the temporary pleasure."

"But I love kissing you." He pulled her to him and his lips found hers again with renewed passion.

She felt herself enjoying his passion more than she knew she should so she backed him off a bit and stopped to catch her breath.

"You're driving me nuts, Emily," he said," and she smiled at him.

He started kissing her again, and she became more aroused than ever before. Before long, she was down in the seat of his car and he was pulling up her skirt. His hand was on her thigh.

"No, Danny," she said. "I can't do this."

"Please, Emily, I need you, I love you," he kept saying as he struggled to loosen her clothing.

He was struggling to get her dress up and was having

some difficulty. It was surrealistic, almost as if she were watching the whole event taking place, and not like she was a participant in it. She felt herself dig her heels into the seat and lift up so he could pull her skirt up over her waist. Then she lowered her panties just enough so he could take them down her legs and toss them onto the seat somewhere.

So, this is what it's like, she thought, and gave up any pretense of resistance.

Afterward, they both had to spend some time catching their breath. When they had straightened their clothing, he kissed her again very passionately, and she returned his kisses with equal passion.

Emily showered as soon as she got home and then barely slept the rest of the night. All night long, she thought about what had happened to her. She supposed that she had become a woman, although she was only sixteen-years-old. It was not the horrible experience she had imagined it would be. In fact, if she were honest, and one is almost always honest with oneself, she really enjoyed it.

The next morning, however, she awoke and hated herself for what she had allowed to happen. The talk would be all over the school now and she would be no different, in the minds of every boy in school, from any of the "easy" girls who were so popular because they were easy. She felt just awful, as awful as she'd ever felt in her life. Her greater concern, however, was that she would get pregnant and that would ruin her life far more quickly than a bad reputation.

When the phone rang and her mother told her it was Danny Miller, Emily felt even worse. She couldn't imagine why he would be calling her now. She answered with much reticence. "Hello," she said,

"Emily, it's Danny, how are you?"

"I'm okay, Danny," she said.

"Emily, I'm really sorry about last night. I hope you can forgive me. You don't know how bad I feel about it. I just love you so much, I couldn't stop, I mean I really needed you. I don't ever want any other girl but you. Nobody knows but you and me and nobody ever will. Just please tell me you'll forgive me."

"There's nothing to forgive, Danny. You didn't force me. Honestly, I wanted to do it too. Thank you for not telling anyone. I don't think we should see each other for a while. We took a big chance, and I cannot risk getting pregnant."

"I know and I'll use protection next time, I promise. I hope you change your mind on that, Emily. I'll go crazy if I can't see you."

"We'll see each other at school, I just mean we shouldn't date for a while."

"I hope you won't do that. I don't want to break it off altogether. I do love you, and I can't wait until you get back from college to see you again."

"I don't know where I'll be going to school, Danny. I

might go somewhere in Vermont. If that happens, then it won't be too far away."

"I hope that happens, Emily," he said. "You're the girl I want to marry."

It was that comment that brought her back into the real world. She could not imagine now that she would ever come back to Middlebury and marry Danny Miller.

CHAPTER 2

Casey

The Boulder Bar and Grill was an upscale night spot at the corner of Broadway and Mapleton Avenue in Boulder, Colorado. It began doing business at that location in the year 2000 and, in just a few years, had become one of the most popular gathering places in Boulder and the surrounding area. Catering to every demographic in the county. Most nights, and especially the weekends, would find the establishment filled with college kids, businessmen and women, construction workers, and even families who often came just for the great food.

The manager of the BBG, as it was locally identified, was a congenial, but imposing, man named Martin Seymour who had been running the place for two years. Seymour was a tall man, about six-feet-three but not heavy. Strong muscular arms helped him move beer kegs around and up into their slots under the bar, like they were nothing at all. One busy night, Martin spotted one of his employees, a young college kid named Billy, trying to set one of the beer kegs into its slot under the bar.

"Let me get that, Billy," Martin said. He took hold of the keg, squatted under it, and hoisted it up into place.

"Thanks, boss," Billy said.

Most of the help were college girls who worked part-time and on weekends. There were a few full-time employees. The cooks were almost all Hispanics and the bartenders were mostly older men and women but most of the waitresses were from the university.

"How can you work around all these beautiful women, Martin, and not go insane?" an occasional customer or vendor would ask him.

"You become desensitized to it," Martin would say. "It's just a job, although it does beat working on a construction site with a bunch of ugly men."

One busy night, a young man approached Martin and asked him if he was the manager. "Yes, I am, sir," Martin replied. "How can I help you?"

"Well, sir, my name is Case MacNicol and I'm having dinner here tonight with my grandpa and his housekeeper. It's her birthday and she has been working for us over twenty years, so I was hoping you could have your girls come by and sing 'Happy Birthday' to her. I'd like to surprise both of them."

"We can certainly do that, Mister MacNicol," Martin replied. "What's her name?"

'Oh no, Mister MacNicol is my grandpa. Call me Case, and her name is Lupita."

"Fair enough, Case, if you will call me Martin."

"I will," he said. "Thank you, Martin, I appreciate it.

A short while later, a bevy of eight beauties surrounded the MacNicols' table. One of them set a small cake, with one candle in it, down on the table in front of Lupita and the rest sang the song to her. Lupita giggled and James MacNicol clapped his approval. Case stood up and thanked the girls.

"You come back anytime, doll," one of them told him. "My name is Angie, ask for me."

"I'll remember that, Angie," he said." Thanks again for what you guys did." He handed her three one-hundred-dollar bills. "Keep one of these for yourself and divide up the other two between your helpers."

"Holy shit!" she exclaimed. Thank you, sir." She almost swooned.

"Case, call me Case," he said.

"God, is he good looking?" she said to the others when she got back to the waitress station.

"Who is that guy, Angie?" one of them asked her.

"I don't know but I've got to find out. He gave us a three-hundred-dollar tip for singing happy birthday to his grandmother. That's almost forty bucks apiece. The guy must be loaded."

"His name is Case MacNicol," Martin said, over-hearing their conversation, and he is loaded, according to Bobby Flores in the kitchen. Bobby claims to know him. He owns a ranch outside of town with his grandfather. And the lady is not his grandmother, she's their house-keeper."

"Well, I've got to get into those Levis with him, that's all I know. Oh, I'm sorry, Martin. I guess I was thinking out loud," Angie said.

"No problem, Angie," he replied, "just don't assault him on company property. Let him make the first move."

That brought laughter from his waitresses.

"Is it okay if I dream about him, boss?"

"As long as you do it on your own time, Angie," Martin said, laughing.

To Martin's surprise and delight, Case showed up again at the BBG one Friday night. Tagging along beside him was an attractive woman, a strawberry blonde with shoulder length hair, brown eyes, and substantial breasts.

"Hello, Martin," Case said as he reached out and shook Martin's hand. "This is a friend of mine, Andrea."

"Hi, Andrea," Martin said, and he shook her hand.

There was no escaping the angst she felt at being re-ferred to as a "friend" of Case's. He watched her make that complaint to him as they were led to a table by the hostess.

"I would think that, after as many times as you've screwed me, you could refer to me as something more than a friend, Case MacNicol." She was fuming.

"I'm sorry, Andrea, should I have said 'good friend' because you are good?"

"You're an asshole."

"Now I gave you a complement, and you're mad about it. Okay, what do you want me to call you?

"Am I not your girlfriend by now? Do I not get at least that much respect from you? I should just tell you to go screw your Llamas and forget about you."

"They're alpacas," he said, smiling at her.

"Oh, what the hell is the difference? Don't answer that, I don't really care. Go screw your alpacas."

"Well, they're not as pretty as you are but neither do they complain as much as you do. They don't drink and all they eat is hay and alfalfa. It would be a cheap date but alpacas are too short. I like taller women."

"That's right, make a joke out of it. You don't care how I feel."

"Aw now, that's not true. Come here." He pulled her chair over next to his, leaned over, and kissed her long and passionately. "I'm sorry, Andrea, I really didn't mean to hurt your feelings. I was just playing with you. Forgive me?"

"Damn you, you know I will and I know we'll end up in bed tonight just like always."

"Nah, I've got a busy day tomorrow so I won't be able to make it tonight."

"You better be joking, Case," she yelled at him.

Several other girls came over to their table. One was Andrea's roommate, Kim and the others were from the dormitory in which Andrea and Kim also had a room. They also kept an apartment for parties and for meeting guys they could not take to the dorm.

The five girls hovered around Andrea's table, wanting to get a glimpse of Case and to be introduced.

"These are my friends from the dorm, honey," she told Case.

She named them off one by one. And he stood up and shook hands with them. Then they went and sat down as the band of the night started playing. The music was typically loud. Whether it was country or soft rock and roll, it was always loud so that talking was kept to a minimum until the band took breaks.

A stunning young waitress, with long black hair and beautiful brown eyes, came to check their order.

"You're Angie, right?" Case asked the girl.

"You remembered. I'm impressed. Yes, Angie, it is. Can I get you guys anything?"

"I want to move to the tables where my friends are, Case," Andrea said, ignoring the waitress.

"I can do that for you, Case," Angie said, ignoring Andrea. "Let me get some more chairs and an extra table."

In a moment, Andrea was amongst her friends, where she could show off her "catch" and flaunt him to the rest of them.

They were barely seated when Andrea's best friend, Kim got up and came over to Case. "Will you dance with me, Case?" she asked him.

"Sure, Kim, come on." He took her hand and, before Andrea could protest, they were on the dance floor. "You're a good dancer, Kim. I'll try not to step on your feet."

"You can step anywhere on me you want to, Case."

"And why would I do that?"

"I'm just being silly 'cause you're so good looking," Kim said.

"You're not so bad looking yourself."

"Thank you, but I'm not Andrea."

"No, there is only one Andrea," he said, "and thank goodness for that."

"I've always wanted to do it with a cowboy."

"I'm not a cowboy, I raise alpacas. And don't you dare call me an alpaca boy or this dance is over right now."

She laughed out loud, and Andrea glared at the both of them. "Will you do it with me, Case?"

When he was a few years younger, he would have been shocked at her directness but he'd come to expect such from women these days. It was just the way things were.

"I can't, Kim. Andrea and I are dating, and I just don't think it's honest to double dip like that. Besides, she's your friend."

"But you're not in a committed relationship, and I know you've been sleeping together because she never shuts up about it. Please, Case, I'll come to your place. No one will know."

"Someone always knows, Kim. I'm sorry, I can't. It's not that you're not attractive, you are, but I just can't."

The music ended and they went back to the table. Andrea could tell by Kim's demeanor that something was up. Case figured that Kim would tell her that he had tried to put a move on her. The fur would fly, and he would be right in the middle of it before it was over.

The band took a break and the place became quiet. Andrea's gang began chattering like a bunch of magpies, as his grandfather often described talkative women. There was Mara, the redhead; Lana; Crystal; Josie; and Rachel. They were all attractive in an eerily similar, college girl, sort of way.

Case began hanging out at the BBG more than any other place in Boulder. It was not for the abundance of "easy" women, it was because he had found a friend in Martin Seymour.

"I don't have many friends, Martin, actually that's a lie, I don't have any friends."

"Aw. Cry me a river, Case. You have friends that

men would kill you for if they thought they could get away with it."

"Yeah, but they don't make me happy," Case said.

"I can see how miserable you are every time you walk out of here with some foxy little tight-ass."

"You ever try to have an actual conversation with one of them."

"No," Martin said, emphatically, leaving no room for discussion on the subject.

Case laughed at his abruptness. "Well, I guess that makes you smarter than me. How did you get to be manager of this place, Martin? I mean, this place looked like it was about to go under a couple of years ago. Then, all of a sudden, it started booming. I heard it had a new manager. I came in to see who it was and discovered it was you. You must have your shit together. Tell me how you did it, one businessman to another."

"I had a thing for Colorado long before I actually came out here. I went to a trade school to learn restaurant management. This was back in Indiana where I'm from. I worked in restaurants all my working life. But I just wasn't happy. I got married and made a pretty good living but I always wanted more. I started applying for management jobs with restaurant franchise owners all around the country and finally got a bite from the company that owns the BBG. This was in 2011. They hired me as an assistant manager, there were three of us, and it was clear that we were competing for the top job."

"Did they tell you they were looking to promote someone to full manager?" Case asked him.

"They did. A man named, Jimmy McElroy, from corporate was running the place and he wanted to get back home to Atlanta so he made it clear that he was going to promote one of us early in 2012, 'come hell or high water,' as he put it."

"Nothing like creating harmony between employees by telling them they are all competing for the same job."

"Tell me about it," Martin said. "So, McElroy, gave us different areas to manage for two months at a time, and then switched around. Then he gauged our performance somehow and made a decision."

"So how did he decide on you?"

"I don't know for sure. I guess my numbers looked better than the others. Why do you think he did it, Case?"

"What do you mean? Oh, you mean do I think they gave it to you because you're black and the other guys were white, and the company is based in Atlanta?"

"That's what the other two guys thought."

"Well, these days, it's damned near impossible to find a place to put a vehicle in your parking lot, any day of the week. You have every demographic all over the scale in here on any given night. From your typical yuppie families to college kids and rednecks, and everybody gets along. So, I'd say it doesn't make a shit what the other two dishwashers thought. Maybe Mister McElroy was just a bottom-line corporate bean-counting type of shmuck."

"Well, you certainly have a way with words, Case MacNicol," Martin said and they both laughed. "Now tell me what you do"

"I own an alpaca ranch with my grandpa. You remember we were in here that night with his housekeeper? You sent some girls over to sing 'Happy Birthday' to her."

"Yes, I do remember, you danced with her later. Everyone got a big kick out of that."

"That's become kind of a tradition with us. Lupita raised me after my parents were killed in a car wreck."

"I'm sorry to hear that, Case."

"My dad was named Casey and he worked with my grandpa in the early days of the ranch. When he married my mother, they built an apartment on the side of the barn. It had one large bedroom, a living room, a full kitchen, and bath with a washer and dryer. When I came along in 1990, they set up a small bed in their bedroom. They called me Case to distinguish me from my dad. After he died, the name stuck, except with Lupita. She still calls me Casey. In 1995, tragedy struck our family, as I mentioned. My mom and dad were killed in a car wreck while returning from a skiing vacation in Aspen. Grandpa was devastated but he had a five-year-old grandson to take care of, and he had precious little time to grieve for his son and daughter-in-law. He moved me into the main house where Lupita could watch me while he worked the ranch."

"Damn, I'm sorry to hear that, Case."

"Thank you. It hit my grandpa pretty hard. He bought the ranch in 1982, didn't know shit about raising alpacas but he learned how to do it. I'll have you come out and have dinner one evening when you can shake free from this place. Lupita is a great cook."

"I look forward to that, Case."

They made that happen about a week later. Martin showed up at Magnolia Road Ranch one after noon about six o'clock. Case was waiting to meet him just inside the gate to run interference between him and the two dogs.

"They're not as mean as they look, Martin," Case said, as Martin got off his bike and took off his helmet,

"They're beautiful dogs, but I have a theory about dogs. If they have teeth, they'll bite."

"Well, they won't bite you as long as I'm here. Anyway, say hello to Bogey and Bacall. They're our 'first responders.' They take care of the 'pacas."

Martin held out his hand for the dogs to sniff and they started wagging their tails. "Oh, the tails are wagging, we're okay then."

"Yep," Case said, "you got past the easy part, now let's go meet my grandpa." He laughed at the look on Martin's face. "I'm kidding, Martin. Grandpa's an old softy."

They went into the house. "Hey, Grandpa," Case

called out. "This is Martin Seymour, my friend from Boulder I told you about."

"Hello, Martin," James said as he shook Martin's hand. "Come on in. Lupita's getting dinner ready. We can shoot the shit while we're waiting. Oops, I hope my language didn't offend you, Martin."

"I run a bar, Mister MacNicol, I've heard worse than that from my waitresses."

"Yes, I expect you have," James replied, "and call me James."

"Yes, sir, James, I'll do that, thank you, and thank you for having me to dinner."

"It's our pleasure, Martin. You're welcome here anytime. I hope you'll make this a regular thing."

Lupita served dinner—enchiladas, soft tacos, guacamole salad, beans, and rice.

"This is the best Mexican food I've had in Colorado," Martin said.

"Case will get mad at me for saying this," James said, "but I'm going to say it anyway. You got to go to Texas for really good Mexican food."

"I go to Casa Bonita in Denver every so often," Martin said.

James just snarled and shook his head.

"I'm going to give Martin a tour of the ranch, Grandpa," Case said.

"Okay," James said. "Come back to see us Martin. It was good to meet you."

"You too, James, and thank you, Lupita. I really enjoyed the meal."

"Thank you, Senor Martine—" She mispronounced his name. "—you come back here when you want Mexican food, don't go to Casa Bonita."

Case spent an hour showing Martin the alpacas and all the barns and gave him a brief history of the ranch.

The two men became good friends and remained so for many years to come.

CHAPTER 3

Leaving Vermont

Emily was in her room when she heard the phone ringing downstairs. She heard her mother's footsteps going to the phone in the living room and listened for her name to be called.

"Emily, telephone."

They did not have a second phone upstairs so Emily hustled downstairs, expecting it to be Danny Miller, but it wasn't.

"Hello, Miss Quarters, this is Doctor Jason Shelby. I'm with The Burlington Group, in Burlington, Vermont. A couple of years ago I spoke with Doctor Allen Gregory there in Middlebury. He told me that you have been working with your brother who is autistic, and that you have been teaching him to function in the world."

"Yes, Doctor Shelby, I remember Doctor Gregory. I'm still working with Murphy, that's my little brother, and he's getting along very well."

"Good, I'm glad to hear that. Now, Miss Quarters, the reason I'm calling is that we'd like to come to Middlebury and talk to you about a possible career in teaching special needs children. Would it be okay if the director of our school and I come down and visit with you sometime next week?"

"Of course, Doctor, I'd welcome the opportunity, thank you."

"How does around two o'clock next Thursday sound? You aren't taking any summer classes, are you?"

"No, I'm not, Doctor, that day and time will be fine. Do you have my address?"

"If you haven't moved since Doctor Gregory gave it to me."

"No, I'm still in the same location."

"Then we'll see you then."

On that Thursday, Emily heard a car pull drive into the driveway of their house. She ran downstairs and beat her mother to the door. On the stoop, was a man, who looked just like she expected Doctor Shelby to look, and a woman of about fifty-five, whom Shelby introduced as Margaret Winters.

"Please come on in, Doctor and Mrs. Winters. We can sit at the kitchen table, if that's okay. My mother is making some coffee for you and some tea for me. Would either of you prefer tea?"

"Coffee is fine," Shelby said, and Winters nodded.

After they had their tea and coffee in front of them, Shelby smiled at Emily. "We've heard a lot of good things about you, Miss Quarters. Could you tell us a little bit about how you got started working with you brother, Murphy, is it?"

"Yes, his name is Murphy," she replied.

"When did you first notice that Murphy was showing signs that he might be autistic?" Doctor Shelby asked her.

"When he was about three-years-old, Doctor," she said.

"Describe to me some of the things that drew your attention to him."

"Well, even before that age, he didn't smile much. I would play with him and tickle him but he didn't respond in kind, like most babies do. After that, he just didn't interact with us, like most three-year-old kids I've known. I spent most of my free time talking to him and teaching him how to form words. He would watch my mouth as I formed a word, and he'd make the same sounds by copying the way I formed the words with my mouth. It would be an exaggerated form of speaking but that was how he learned to talk."

"It must have been a long and laborious process," Shelby said.

"Yes, it was, but I didn't want to see him have to go

away to a state school. I thought he would be better off here with his family."

"How did you know he had autism?"

"I didn't, I didn't know what it was until I did some research. Even then, I wasn't sure. Once the doctors confirmed it, I knew that I could teach him how to cope. But there is only so much I know how to do. I honestly don't know if I'll be able to help him when he becomes an adult."

"How old are you now, Miss Quarters?" Winters asked her.

"I'm sixteen, ma'am," Emily replied.

Shelby and Winters looked at each other and nodded their heads. "We are going to send you some literature and check on Murphy's progress from time to time, if that's okay with you, Miss Quarters. And may we call you Emily?"

"Of course, Doctor, no one has ever called me Miss Quarters. It kept making me think you were talking to someone else."

They both laughed at that.

"And the literature would be very helpful, Thank you."

They wanted to meet Murphy. Emily brought him downstairs and showed them how she worked with him when she was teaching him words, just as she had shown Doctor Gregory.

"We are going to contact you when you graduate

from high school and have you come to Burlington to discuss where we go from here," Shelby told her.

"Great, Doctor. I look forward to hearing from you," Emily said.

"Just keep those grades up, Emily," Winters said to her as they left the house.

"Definitely, Mrs. Winters, I will."

When they were back in their car, Doctor Shelby just shook his head. "That is one incredible young lady. We are definitely going to want to talk to her when she graduates from high school."

"I couldn't agree more, Jason," Winters replied. "She has a God-given talent that we just don't see very often."

Emily continued teaching Murphy how to speak clearly and how to write. Mostly, he learned to write phonetically but she was able to teach him to write a lot of grammatically correct papers for the stories he liked to put down on paper. All the while, Emily was able to graduate at the top of her high school class. The local newspaper did a piece on her and on her work with an autistic child. Emily became quite a popular personality in Middlebury.

She turned eighteen not long after graduation. She had maintained her 4.0 average and, the day after graduation, she received that call from Burlington. They were asking her to come in and talk to them about a possible career working with their school and hospital facility for special needs children. She borrowed the family car, drove to the facility, and met with the three-member staff. She took all her notes, theories, and copies of the early work that her brother had done, as they had asked her to do. She again met with Doctor Shelby and Mrs. Winters.

"I see you've grown up a bit in two years, Emily," Shelby said, shaking her hand.

"Just a bit, I suppose, Doctor, but you still look the same."

"Well, that makes my day, thank you. I'll get right to business. We'd like to ask you if you would be interested in getting a degree in Special Needs Studies, and in bringing that back to Vermont and using what you know for children here," Shelby said. "In other words, we are offering you a job with a delayed start date. Is that something you might be interested in doing, Emily?"

"It is, Doctor, but my family doesn't have a lot of money. I am planning to apply for an academic scholarship but I don't know how much that will cover. I may have to get a job."

"We can help you with that," Mrs. Winters, the school director said. "Do you have any preference for a school you'd like to go to?"

"No, ma'am, I really haven't thought about it much."

"How would you like to go to Colorado, Emily?"

"I've never been there but I've always wanted to go. Is that a possibility?"

"We have gotten help from the school for a couple of kids in the past. With your credentials, I don't think it will be a problem. The scholarship will provide for your tuition and books. Our school will pay for your room and board. We'll fly you back in the summer and you can work here and earn some spending money for the next school year."

"That sounds too good to be true," Emily said.

"It's not. You just have to decide if you can handle being away from home for the school year for four years in a row. It will be quite a sacrifice. Also, we will want you to sign a contract agreeing to work for us for four years, after you graduate. Can you make that commitment?"

"Yes, I can. It's what I want to do with my life," Emily said.

"Then we'll get the paperwork together for you to start this next school year. It's going to be a lot of hard work for you, Emily, but I have no doubt you can do it," Winters said.

"I think it will be worth it, Mrs. Winters. I'd love to go to school in Colorado."

"Then we will get the ball rolling. You'll need to be ready to leave around the middle of August. Will you fly or do you have a car? It's quite a long trip, you know."

"I don't know yet. I think I'll try to get a car before I go."

"Just let me know. Here's my card. Keep in touch so we can coordinate."

Emily's greater concern was leaving her brother

alone. Murphy was only twelve, and she worried that his progress would suffer if she were not there to tutor him.

Her parents sought to relieve her anxiety regarding her brother's future.

"Emily, we are so proud of what you've done for your brother, and for yourself," Norman told her. "Your mother and I have been remiss in our responsibility to both of you. I want to make that up to you now."

"What do you mean, Dad?"

"We are going to continue working with Murphy like you have done all his life. I know we won't know as much as you do about his condition, but I figure you can help us, over the phone and through email, and if you are willing to do that, we will do everything we can to see that his progress is not impeded."

"That will make me very happy, Dad," she said. "You both will be surprised at what a blessing it will be to all three of you. Murphy is a wonderful boy, and he's smart, Dad, very smart, you'll see."

"I believe you and, even though I hate to see you go so far away, I am so happy for you. Your mother is too. It's almost like you raised us, not the other way around."

"You and Mom are not bad parents. A special needs child can be a terrible burden on a family if you only see the downside."

"But you were able to see the possibilities, Emily, and I love you for it and thank you for the difference you've made in all our lives. You're a special girl."

She went over to him and hugged him. "Thank you, Daddy. I love you too," she said.

She then went to Murphy's room to explain to him why she would be leaving soon. The boy understood the leaving part but did not fully comprehend why his most ardent supporter and friend would no longer be around. He became very emotional. She held him in her arms until he calmed down.

"I won't be gone forever, Murph. I'll be back in the summer to see you and we can email each other. Remember, I showed you how to use the computer, and I set you up an email account. I want you to email me every day, and I will answer you every day and call you on the phone."

"I don't want you to go away, Emmy," he said.

"I know, Murph. I don't want to either but if I go away for a while I will be able to come back and help a lot of people. And that's a good thing, right?"

"Uh huh," he said, nodding his head up and down.

A few days later Emily received a call from Mrs. Winters.

"Miss Quarters, I've made all the necessary arrangements for you to begin classes in the fall. If you can start getting your things together, that would be helpful. Have you decided if you are going to drive or fly to Boulder?"

"I don't know yet. I'm thinking that getting a car would be better so I can take all my things with me and not have to ship them or try to carry a lot of stuff on the plane."

Her dad was ahead of her on that. He drove into the drive way with a 2009 Ford Focus. "It's a used car, Emily—excuse me, it's a previously owned car—but it's in tip-top shape and I had it checked out. It's mechanically sound."

"Oh, Daddy, it's beautiful and my favorite color, blue. I've been so caught up in everything that's been happening that I had no idea how I was going to get to Colorado."

"Well then, I'm glad I could be of service to you. It's paid for and you're on my insurance. Just remember to get it serviced regularly after you get settled in."

"Thank you so much. It's wonderful, I love it."

The next morning, she heard the doorbell ring and could recognize her mother's footsteps going to the door. A few seconds later, her mother called out to her. "Emily, Danny Miller is here to see you."

"Danny Miller," she said out loud and went down the stairs to the door. "Hello, Danny, what do you want?"

"Hi, Emily, your mom told me you were leaving town soon, and I was hoping I could take you to lunch before you go."

"They run out of beer at Jimmy's house?"

"No, I just wanted to see you before you leave. I love you, Emily, you know I do. Can't we just go to lunch? I won't try anything."

"I suppose we can. Come on in and sit down. I have to change."

He took her to a local café on the other side of Otter Creek. "So, you're going to Colorado? Which school are you going to?"

"UC," she told him, "The University of Colorado in Boulder."

"Wow, that's a long way from Middlebury. It's really beautiful out there."

"You've been to Colorado?"

"No, I've never been anywhere. I've never been out of Vermont."

"Neither have I. I never felt the need to go anywhere but Vermont, but now I do, so I'll be leaving in a few days."

"Can I email you? I'd like to stay in touch."

"You can, Danny, but please understand, we're not a couple. What happened between us was just something that happened. I didn't get pregnant, thank God. And it doesn't mean we will never see each other again, but I have a lot on my plate right now. If you want to write me, that's fine. I'm going to be pretty busy so don't expect me to do any online chat or texting. I just won't have time for that."

"Okay, I just want to write you and maybe see you when you come back."

"I'll be back during the summer break and, after I graduate, I'm going to work for a school and hospital facility in Burlington. So, I may see you again. You never know what might happen."

"You're beautiful, Emily."

"No, I'm not," she said, rolling her eyes.

"Yes, you are. I don't know why you can't accept that."

"I don't think I'm beautiful, Danny. I think I'm plain looking."

"Then you're lying to yourself," he insisted. "If you don't take anything else away from the time you've known me, then understand that. You're a beautiful girl. It takes a man's eyes to see it but behind the glasses, the hair, and your refusal to see it yourself, you are beautiful. You are a beautiful girl, a beautiful woman. That's all I'm going to say to you today, and this is the last time I'm going to say it. I'll take you home now."

"Thank you, Danny," she told him as she got out of his car. She was a little surprised that he didn't try to kiss her. "Write me and I'll write back," she said

She hated being so harsh with him but she just didn't want any entanglements. She didn't want him calling her constantly while she was away at school. She wanted a clean break and a fresh start.

She googled the distance from Middlebury to Boulder. "Holy cow," she said out loud. "It's nineteen hundred miles to Boulder." It would take her three days to drive that distance, but at least she would have a car when she got there. The Burlington group had given her a credit card with $2,000 balance for her trip and settling in expenses. She planned to be as frugal as possible so she would have some spending money left over. Her dad said he would send her some money every month, as much as he could.

She mapped out her trip, using Google and Daddy had bought a GPS for her car so she felt confident she could get to Boulder without ending up at the Pacific Ocean. She tried to program the address of the school into her GPS but discovered that it would not accept it until she was physically in the state of destination. So, she would have to rely on her Google directions.

She felt empowered as she finally said her goodbyes to her mom and dad, and to her brother Murphy, and pulled out of the driveway to begin her new life. Through New York and into Ohio, she was breaking new ground, seeing country she'd never seen before. She pulled into a rest stop in Ohio to sleep for a while and curled up in the front seat of her car. Sometime later, a tapping sound awakened her, and she sat up. An Ohio State Trooper was at her window so she turned on the ignition and rolled it down.

"Are you okay, miss?" he asked her.

"Yes, sir," she answered him. "I was tired so I stopped to sleep a while."

"Okay, I just wanted to make sure you weren't hurt or sick."

"No, I'm fine, just tired from driving."

"Where are you headed, miss?"

"Boulder, Colorado, I'm starting to school there this coming semester."

"Wow, you have a long way to go. Okay, sorry to have bothered you. Finish your nap and drive carefully."

"Do you need to see my license and insurance papers?"

"No, miss, that's okay. If anyone messes with you while you're here, just lay on your horn. There's usually a trooper close by, and he'll come check on you."

"Thank you, Officer," she said.

He put his finger to the tip of his hat and smiled at her then turned around and left.

In Indiana, she rented a motel room for the night so she could get a good night's sleep and take a shower in the morning. There was a diner next to the motel so she had breakfast and got back on the road.

When Emily left Illinois, she suddenly felt giddy. At first, she thought it was from road fatigue but it continued half way through Illinois. It was a light-headed, happy feeling that she had rarely experienced in her life. It was a "release," she soon decided. Her entire life had been structured, structured right down to the most intimate detail. She'd planned for this time since she was fourteen-years-old. Working with her brother had been a vision of what her life's work would be.

Emily had a path in life, and she had stuck to that path through middle school, through high school, and now through college she would stick to it. She had not let herself fall into the trap that most kids her age had fallen into. Drinking, partying, having sex, getting pregnant, an early unwanted marriage, and similarly unwanted divorce, that would not be her fate. Hard work and dedication to a goal had paid off for her, and she would not let herself be distracted. Emily Quarters would one day be writing medical manuals on the care and treatment of autism and autistic children. She would lecture to huge audiences worldwide. But for now, she was free, on her own. She giggled as she sped up and went over the speed limit by ten miles per hour for a few minutes then slowed it back down.

She thought for a moment that she might return to Middlebury one day and marry Danny Miller. He had actually been pretty nice to her, and, if she were truthful, if only to herself, she could have stopped him that night when "things went too far" but the honest truth was that she actually enjoyed it. She didn't rave on and on about because she knew he'd want to start doing it on a regular basis, and she was not ready for that sort of relationship with Danny.

A new world awaited her now in Colorado. She had only seen it in pictures, videos, and in movies but, in her mind, it had always been this magical place where dreams come true. She was convinced that her dreams would come true, just as soon as she arrived in Boulder.

She would have to work for it, but she had proven

long ago that she was not afraid of work.

She wondered what the girls in her dorm would be like. She hoped to make at least one friend. She had heard of women who had made friends in college and remained friends until late in life. Emily thought that would make for a nice relationship. Someone to confide in and lean on in trying times, to have over for coffee, or to fly across the country to visit every so often would be really good element to have in one's life.

She also wondered how it would affect her life should she meet a man. She had heard that many girls went to college to snag a husband. That was not her intent but what if she met someone and fell in love? She had no clue what that would feel like. She didn't love Danny Miller, she barely even liked him very much. Danny was a boy, though. One day she hoped to meet a man, a real man. Would he be someone like her, inexperienced in the game of love and affairs of the heart? Only time would tell what awaited her in Colorado.

She stopped at a roadside café in Des Moines, Iowa, to eat lunch. An older woman with a nametag that identified her as 'Sal' came to her table.

"Hi, sweetie, here's a menu. What can I get you to drink?"

"I'll have water to drink, ma'am," Emily said.

The waitress nodded. "I'll be back in just a minute to get your order."

Emily ordered a club sandwich and, in just a short

while, Sal brought it to her table. "Where you headed, darlin'?" she asked, smiling at Emily.

"Colorado, Boulder," Emily responded.

"I bet you're going to the university there, aren't you?"

"I am, how did you know that?"

"You look like a college kid. You look like you're very smart too. Are you smart? Oh, silly me. No one is going to say they are smart. That would be arrogant. What are you going to be studying?"

"I'm majoring in the education and care of special needs children, primarily autistic children," Emily said.

"Well then, you answered my question for me. You must be smart. You have to be smart to do all that," the waitress said.

"Thank you..." Emily quickly looked at her name tag. "...thank you, Sal."

"Well, you are quite welcome, dear. I wish you the best of luck out there."

"Thank you for that, too," Emily told her, then she paid her bill, used her cell phone calculator to figure how much tip to leave Sal, and she was back on her way.

Another nap in a rest stop in Nebraska and again in Eastern Colorado and, all of a sudden, the Rocky Mountains came into view.

Emily was awestruck. She had seen pictures of the mountains, and they had mountains in Vermont, but those mountains were foothills compared to what she was seeing now. The mountains grew bigger the closer she got to Boulder and then, all of a sudden, they were gone, hidden behind the foothills.

She drove around the town for a while before she went to her designated dorm.

"This is the coolest town I've ever been in," she said out loud and got excited just being there. "This is going to be fun," she continued, talking to herself as she drove around the town.

Emily was going to blossom here. She already felt at home.

She called her folks. "I'm here, Mom. I just got into town. I've been driving around, checking things out before I go to my dorm. It's absolutely breathtaking. I wish you could see it."

"I'm excited for you, Emily. I'll tell your dad that you arrived safely. Write us every day, honey, and call when you can."

Emily promised she would.

When she got to her dorm, she was told that some new construction that was done over the summer was not yet completed, and that they were going to assign her to another dormitory. She would have a single room since that was all that was available in Baker Hall. While Emily was glad to have a room to herself, she had sort of hoped for a roommate that might become a new friend. The other girls were friendly enough but most of them in her area seemed to be more given to partying than to their studies. That would not deter her, of course. Emily Quarters was on a mission, a mission to be the very best in her field.

CHAPTER 4

Meeting Emily

It was a typical Friday night at the BBG. When Case walked into the place with Andrea, she spotted her gang at their usual table against the wall. Martin had started reserving it for them until a certain time. If a number of them had not arrived by seven o'clock on a weekend night, then he went ahead and let other patrons have it. But on this night, they were there. Case pulled a chair out for Andrea and noticed a new girl at the far end of the table. Mara was waving to him to come to that end of the table, and he did.

"Case, this is Emily. She's new to our dorm. Emily, this is Case MacNicol. You've most likely heard the other girls talking about him."

Case rolled his eyes when she said that, and Emily smiled.

"Hello, Emily," he said and reached for her hand.

She extended hers and, when he shook her hand, he found that her grip was stronger than he'd expected. She didn't just lay her hand out to be taken, she shook his in return. Their eyes met, and he couldn't look away for a few moments. He was inexplicably drawn to her eyes. They were an alluring bright blue, he suddenly realized. She seemed not the least bit intimidated nor inclined to divert her eyes away from his. To his surprise, he became a bit nervous.

"Ah," he said, "you have an impressive handshake, Emily."

"So, do you, Case," she said and smiled at him.

He returned to his seat but kept glancing at her, hoping to catch her eye again, but she didn't glance back at him. *Is she being coy?* he wondered, *or does she really not give a shit about me?* It was a strange experience for him to feel interest in a woman and for the woman not to return that interest. *She's playing games*, he decided, *that has to be it*.

At around ten o'clock, Andrea was ready to leave. "Let's go to my apartment and do it," she said to Case, loudly enough for several of her friends to hear. "I'm horny."

"Can you give Emily a lift back to the dorm, Andrea?" Mara asked. "She has a Saturday class in the morning and doesn't want to stay up all night. We're not ready to leave yet."

"I'd be glad to give her a ride," Case answered for Andrea.

Emily stood up and Case got a better look at her. Her sweater was a couple sizes too large and he wondered if that was an intentional decision on her part to hide her breasts. She wore a matching skirt that fit her body well and ended just above her knees. She was very shapely, there was no question about that, but she apparently made no effort to advertise it.

Andrea was not happy with the inconvenience but she chose not to make a scene. In the parking lot, Case opened the door and Andrea got in first then, Emily got in next to the window. "I don't know where your dorm is so you'll have to tell me how to get there," he said.

"It's the same dorm Andrea lives in but I'll give you directions anyway."

When they arrived at the dorm, he pulled up to the curb, got out, went around, and opened the door for her.

"I'm sorry for the bother but thank you for the lift," she said.

"It was no bother. I'll walk you to the door just for your safety. Let me take your hand," he said, as they walked to the door of the dorm. "I want to make sure you don't stumble"

Andrea seethed in the truck while all this was going on.

He and Emily locked gazes again, and he became mesmerized by her eyes. *What is going on here?* he asked himself.

He couldn't stop looking into those eyes, and he was acting downright stupid over this girl he didn't even know yet. He was transfixed on her eyes, and she seemed in no hurry to break the spell.

He knew he could not stay there much longer, staring into those captivating eyes, so he threw up his arms and shook his head like he was confused. "Okay," he said. "What did I tell you my name was?"

She began laughing. "Oh, come on, Case," she said, beaming. "They're just blue eyes."

"They're more than just blue eyes, Emily. I don't know what yet but I do know that."

He went to sleep that night, thinking about Emily. He didn't even know her last name but there was something about her he couldn't get out of his head.

The next morning, Case was up early, dressed, and headed out of the bedroom when Andrea woke up. "Where are you going?" she asked him.

"Work," he said.

"Will I see you tonight?"

"Maybe. If I come to town, you will," he said.

"I can make you some breakfast."

"No time, we've got a big day today, gotta go. It's shearing week," he lied.

They only sheared the 'pacas once a year but he used

that as an excuse whenever he needed time away from Andrea or whichever woman he was trying to avoid at the time.

"Dammit," she said to herself as she heard the front door of her apartment close. She was still fuming when her roommate Kim woke up and made coffee.

"That man is driving me crazy," she said to Kim.

"You mean Case?"

"Who else would I mean? He's such an asshole, so inconsiderate."

"Let me have him," Kim said. "I wouldn't care how he acted as long as he took me to bed when I asked him."

"Yeah, I know you would. You danced with him the other night right under my nose with no consideration of how it would make me feel."

"Oh, come on, Andrea. That man doesn't belong to you. Case MacNicol doesn't belong to any woman. He'll screw anything with a heartbeat."

"I know, and he gave a ride to that new girl without even asking me if I minded. Then he walked her to the door of the dorm. Holding her hand."

"Really?" Kim said, surprised. "She doesn't seem at all like the kind Case would go for."

"I think he was just dong it to piss me off."

"That had to be it," Kim said, nodding her head.

After leaving Andrea's apartment and arriving at the ranch, Case went to find his grandfather.

"I'm sorry for being late, Grandpa, I overslept," Case

said as he approached his grandfather at the shearing barn.

James chuckled. "Is that what they're calling it these days?"

Case looked sheepishly at him and shrugged his shoulders. He thought about trying to offer an alternate explanation but decided against it. "I'm sorry," he said again.

"It's okay, son. I wasn't exactly a model of virtue when I was your age." His grandfather was philosophic about it. "You'll get hurt one day, son."

"Do you really believe that, Grandpa?" Case responded.

"I know so, Case. It's a universal law. If you continue treating women like they are nothing more than playthings, then one day you will meet one you can't live without, and she'll break your heart."

"I haven't met her yet," Case said, defensively, but his mind's eye suddenly saw those blue eyes again.

"I know that. Do you want to know how I know?"

"Tell me, Grandpa, how do you know?"

"You've never brought one of them home to where you live," James MacNicol said. "I know you're not ashamed of this place or of me, at least I hope that's not the problem. That's a part of your life you're just not ready to share with a woman."

"I'm not ashamed of anything about my life here. I just haven't met a woman I wanted to meet you. I might someday or I might not. I really hope you're right."

"I am right, son. Your father was a lot like you are now until he met your mother. Then he turned into a—"

"Into a wimp?" Case said.

"Into a real man, I was going to say. He changed and, from then on until he died, he was a good husband and a good father. I only wish you could have grown up knowing him. He was a good man, Case."

"I remember him, Grandpa, not much but a little. I remember my mother more because I was always with her. I wish I'd known him too but I'm damned lucky I had you."

"I'm the lucky one, son. I couldn't have done all this without you. I know you are irresponsible where women are concerned, but you're always here when I need you. I appreciate that, I really do."

He started leading the animals from the holding pen to the stalls where they were fed. He had to take the rest of the wool, from the last shearing, into town. They used a flat-bed trailer with high side rails to transport the wool to the spinner/processor in Denver. It would take several trips to take the last batch of product to the processor. Case wanted to get started right away. He backed his truck up to the loaded trailer and the hired hands attached it. He was on his way into Denver when he got a call from Andrea, and she was in a foul mood.

"Where have you been?" she shrieked. "I've been calling you for the last three days."

"Working. I told you it was shearing week, and I would be out of touch for a few days."

"No, when you left you said you had to work that day. You didn't say anything about all week or three days. I've been worried about you."

"I'm sorry," he said. "I thought I had told you, I meant to."

"You're always sorry, after the fact. I swear Case, you're so irresponsible. I get so tired of putting up with your childish bullshit."

"Then don't, Andrea."

"What do you mean?" she asked him.

"Don't put up with it. You don't have to. My business always comes first. It has to. I made that commitment to my grandfather. Tell me to take a hike, and I'll leave you alone."

"I believe you really would."

"If that's what you want," he told her.

"No, it's not what I want and you know it. I'm sorry. Dammit Case, you hurt me all the time, and I always end up apologizing."

"I'll be at the BBG tonight if you want me to pick you up."

"No, I'm going to hang out with some friends at the mall tonight. Maybe I'll see you tomorrow night."

"Okay," he said. "Have fun, I'll be there if you change your mind."

At the BBG the only one of Andrea's gang who was

there was her roommate Kim. Case grimaced as he saw her because he knew she'd be around his neck before too long. He went to the bar, hoping to avoid her. "Coors light," he told the bartender.

Kim was there before the beer was, glomming on to his arm. "Where you been, Case? I missed you."

"I've been working, Kim. Why aren't you with Andrea at the mall?"

"I don't need to do any recreational shopping, and I don't need any comfort food."

"Andrea depressed again?"

"She's all bummed out over you," Kim said and shrugged.

"And shouldn't you be with your friend in her time of need?"

"I was hoping you'd be here and would dance with me."

"I'll dance with you."

"Really?" she said with glee. "Oh my gosh, Case, that's awesome. I'll put some money in the juke box."

"You're a good dancer, Kim, and you're a good-looking woman. But why do you think you have to throw yourself at men the way you do? You must know a lot of men who would love to take you out."

"I don't throw myself at men, Case. I just throw myself at you because you won't have anything to do with me."

"I don't need a steady girlfriend, Kim. Andrea is not

even a girlfriend. We just hang out together quite a bit."

"Andrea doesn't think that, she thinks you belong to her."

"I don't belong to anyone," he said and looked down at her. She was a pretty girl. He'd not really noticed her much before but she was quite striking actually. "What do you want from me, Kim?"

"I want you to make love to me, Case. I'm not telling you that I'm in love with you or that I want a steady dating thing. It's just physical. You're so damned sexy, I dream about you. I need you to make love to me."

"Is Andrea at your apartment?"

Kim's eyes lit up when he asked her that. "No, she's still mad at me for dancing with you the other night so she's staying at the dorm."

Case said nothing. He took her hand and led her off the dance floor, out the door of the bar, and helped her into his truck.

In her room, she was out of her clothes and into bed so fast that he almost started laughing. He took a little longer to get undressed, as if he was teasing her.

"Hurry up, Case," she said, giggling and kicking her legs like a little girl.

He ended up spending the night, got up early, and showered. When he kissed her goodbye, she kissed him with much passion. They started kissing again and couldn't stop. He pulled away for a moment. "Uh-oh," he said.

"Do me again, Case," she pleaded with him.

He looked down into her doleful brown eyes. "Oh, what the hell?" he said and started taking off his clothes.

When he told her goodbye again, she held his head like she didn't want to let go. "You are freaking incredible, Case. Thank you."

"You are too, Kim. And you're quite welcome, thank 'you.' I'm not kissing you again because I really do have to get to work."

Now all he had to do was wait for the shit storm that would surely come when Kim told Andrea about their night together.

He wanted to kick his own ass. He vacillated from, being pleased with himself that he could so effortlessly get a good-looking woman in bed, to feeling like he was not much better than a dog on the prowl. In high school, he reveled in his ego but, as he grew older, he had begun to question the morality of his life-style. He questioned it but he felt no inclination to change it.

His grandfather always wanted Case to go to college but Case had no desire to do that.

"You can go to CU, Case, and live at home," James had often suggested.

"I don't want to go to college, Grandpa," Case always replied. "I can learn everything I need to know on the internet."

"I don't understand all that. I just think you need to get an education, son."

"You didn't go to college and look at what you've done."

"That's different."

"It's really not. I love what we do here, Grandpa. I love the ranch, I love the mountains. I love the work. Hell, I even love these nasty little bastards," Case said, pointing at the alpacas.

"Why do you say they're nasty?"

"They shit a lot. They're always shitting."

"All animals shit, Case, half the problems with any ranching business is getting rid of the manure. And if you haven't noticed, people do too. Aw, hell, I brought out some porta-potties for them but they wouldn't use 'em. At least alpacas all shit in a communal dump."

Case started laughing at his grandfather's joke, delivered with such seriousness that one could almost believe he had actually done that. The older MacNicol man was an icon for an "old timer." He'd never caught up to the modern world and didn't seem much compelled to do so. When his wife Amy died, after Case's parents were killed, James withdrew into himself and never made much effort to come out.

James MacNicol only loved two people in the entire world, his grandson Case and his housekeeper Lupita. His relationship with the latter was as contentious as it was congenial. Many visitors to the ranch thought the two of them were married, but their relationship was platonic and respectful. He yelled and blustered at her and she brushed him off like he was an unruly child.

"Andrea's Angels," as the six girls who made up her following at the BBG were often referred to, lived in Baker Hall on the University of Colorado campus. Three of the girls, Mara, Lana, and Crystal shared a three-bed room and Josie and Rachel lived in a two-bed room. Kim and Andrea also rented a two-bed room for which Andrea's father paid, with some grumbling because she also insisted on his paying for a two-bedroom apartment near the campus. The apartment was ostensibly for the use of her parents on the rare occasions when they came to visit her from Virginia.

It was into this "gaggle" of girls that Emily Quarters was inserted when her room at the other dorm had experienced construction problems.

Emily settled into a single room which was comfortable for her, being a more studious person than the others. They were in college mainly to party and find a husband with a promising career ahead of him.

Mara Jernigan befriended Emily and took it upon herself to shield her as much as was possible from the backbiting politics of Andrea and Kim and some of the other girls.

She learned that Emily was studying to be a teacher and counselor to special needs children. She had a brother who was autistic and she had been sponsored by a school back in Vermont, where her family lived, for her education, on the contingency that she come home and work for the sponsoring school for a certain number of years.

Emily was not flashy, and not as desperate to get a man as the other girls. She had light brown hair that just barely touched her shoulders. The hair was cut in such a fashion that it covered her forehead and part of her face most of the time, making it difficult to see what she actually looked like. She wore round glasses that hid her brilliant blue eyes. She was five feet, four inches tall and weighed no more than 120 pounds. She often dressed frumpy. But Mara noticed some more attractive dresses hanging in her closet. She wore baggy sweaters a lot that kept her breasts from becoming a distraction.

"This is the 'I want a piece of Case MacNicol' wing of the dormitory," Mara explained to Emily.

Emily looked confused. "What is it with Case Mac-Nicol?" she asked.

"The guy who shook your hand and flirted with you the other night at the BBG. You remember, don't you? He's Andrea's boyfriend."

"Oh, I remember him," Emily said. "He told me I had a good handshake or something like that. I just don't know what makes him tick."

"Nobody knows what makes him tick," Mara said.

"What did you think of him? He's gorgeous, isn't he?" Crystal joined in.

"He's pretty enough, I suppose," Emily answered, "but I wouldn't want him."

"Are you kidding me, why not?"

"Too superficial. I think, he's got birddog written all over him."

"Oh, but he's 'so' good looking," Crystal said. "You're right though about the birddog part. He's been with a lot of girls. Nobody knows for sure how many. He never keeps one for very long though, and he never takes anyone to that ranch he claims to have, not even Andrea. She's practically begged him to take her out there to meet his family but he just never has."

"He's been 'doing' Andrea for a couple of months now. It's about time he moved on, I'm guessing," Josie chimed in.

"Josie always takes the conversation to the lowest common denominator," Mara explained to Emily.

"So, he's a cowboy?" Emily said.

"No, it's an alpaca ranch. It's true about the ranch because Case is good friends with Martin, the manager of the BBG, and Martin has been to the ranch. Case owns it with his grandfather. Case is as rich as he is good-looking."

"Alpacas," Emily muttered, as she headed off to her room to study.

But for all her bold talk, she could not fool herself and had to admit that, when the guy stared into her eyes, she felt something tingle in her stomach. It was a slight burning and fluttering. Then, when he walked her to the dorm door, it happened again. He was indeed gorgeous, but she detected honesty in his face that belied his reputation. She wouldn't waste time analyzing him, though. Chances were good she would never see him again.

CHAPTER 5

Magnolia Road Ranch

Red Rudy was Case's prized Huacaya "show" 'paca. He'd won top prize the last two years in the local Colorado competitions, and Case had aspirations of taking him to the nationals in Ohio and Massachusetts. His grandfather was not as enamored with the competition circuits as was his grandson.

"Waste of money," James MacNicol always exclaimed when Case began hinting about showing Rudy. "They're not pets, Case, they're business."

"But, Grandpa, they draw a lot of attention to the industry. After every show, there is an increased demand for alpacas for pets and for stuff made from the wool. When Rudy took first place last year in Denver, the alpaca apparel outlet sold out in a day. We couldn't keep enough product on the shelves."

"And how much money did we make off of all that?"

"I don't know, Grandpa, but I'm guessing quite a bit."

"Quite a bit, eh? Is that what I tell the accountant, quite a bit?"

Case started laughing. "Okay, Grandpa. I should have learned by now that I need my facts and figures together before I start a debate with you."

The old man had run the ranch for thirty-three years. Case was convinced that his grandpa had only hired an accountant because of the convoluted tax system. He believed that only accountants knew enough about it to be able to bullshit people into believing they knew what they were talking about. James MacNicol could manage the entire business in his head, were it not for the taxes he had to pay on the income generated from the ranch.

Case's earliest memories of his grandfather included riding the pony he'd bought for Case when he was only five or six and trying to keep up with the older man, as they roamed the hills and valleys to the west of the ranch. Sometimes, they would ride to the top of the mountain to the southwest and camp overnight. They'd sit on a rock overhang and watch the sun come up and wash over the Front Range. Case inherited his grandfather's love for Colorado, and he never imagined that he'd ever leave permanently, no matter what the reason might be. It was his home and he felt blessed to have been born in this wonderful place.

In the distance to the south, on a clear day, they could see Pikes Peak. "I'll take you there when you get a little older," James had told him. And he did when Case was twelve years old. They took a trip to Colorado Springs and drove up to the summit.

"This is like driving into heaven, Grandpa, are we in the clouds?"

"Sometimes it's sunny here but the clouds roll in usually before you get time to enjoy the sun. At least that's the way it's been every time I've been here. I used to bring your daddy here in the summer when he was a boy."

"What was he like, Grandpa?"

"He was a lot like you, Case, a good boy, and he turned into a good man. I expect you will be a lot like him. But your dad didn't have rancher's blood running through his veins like you do. He was very smart. He started an investment account for you when you were born. It will be available for you to use to go to college, if you want to. If you don't go to college, you'll be able to have it when you are twenty-five. There's a substantial amount of money in it, and your dad was smart enough to stipulate that you had to be twenty-five before you get the money. He didn't want you pissing it away on frivolous things."

"What was my mother like?"

"She was a very pretty woman but she talked too much. Some women are like that."

"Oh, tell me about it. Girls at school never stop talking. They don't even slow down. You know what I mean?"

"Indeed, I do, son. Please don't grow up and marry a ratchet-jaw. You'll be miserable all your life."

"What's a ratchet-jaw, Grandpa?"

"That's like one those girls you were talking about. Marry a quiet woman, Case. She may set you on fire when you're asleep in your bed some night but at least she won't talk you to death."

"You're funny, Grandpa. I love you."

"I love you too, son. Listen, Case, that was all in fun. Seriously, though, your mother was a wonderful woman, and she made your dad happy. He loved her very much. It was hard losing them both."

"What happened to Grandma?" Case asked.

"Losing your father was just too much for Amy. She had a heart attack after we got the news about the accident. I wanted to die too but I had to look after you. I thank God for you because you've made everything we've done on the ranch possible. If I had not had you, I would have just withered away to nothing."

Case MacNicol grew up and came to respect the wisdom his grandfather had acquired in all his years. James had sought to pass it all on to his grandson. Most of it took, but learning wisdom—having the learned knowledge—and applying it and letting it guide your heart were often two very different things.

Case had natural good looks and an endearing charm which he perfected with much determination as he grew up. He was an imperfect cad, unapologetically using women for his own benefit, but he never ridiculed or belittled a woman. If he ever unintentionally hurt a woman's feelings, he was quick to apologize. When a relationship ended, though a woman might be heartsick and wondering what went wrong, they never hated Case nor did they wish harm to come to him in any way. They were left with an empty hole that, at that time, they thought could never be filled again. Love given by a woman to Case MacNicol was wasted love. But none of them ever wished they'd never met him.

"You know, Case," James MacNicol said. "I've never told you this but I often pondered how much different our lives would have been if your mom and dad had not been killed so early in their lives. I've never been a religious man but I asked God why that happened, many times. I never got an answer that would put the matter to rest in my mind. I visited and revisited every moment of my life, trying to recall what terrible sin I might have committed that warranted such judgement from the Almighty, but, in my own estimation, while not being a perfect human being by any measuring stick, I could not bring myself to believe that I had ever been a threat to society, of such magnitude, that I should be thusly crippled in my pursuit of life, liberty, and happiness."

"Shit just happens, Grandpa, doesn't mean you're a bad person."

"That's what I finally decided, Case. I eventually had to come to grips with the simple truth that things happen in life that there is just no explanation for. The hand of God didn't just reach down and strike me for some imagined offensive against heaven or mankind, it had just happened. My son was gone and my son's wonderful wife, Hannah. Hannah had brought a light to the ranch even before she gave us a son. Then all I had left was you, five years old and full of life and wonder."

"I remember my mother vaguely but mostly I remember you teaching me how to ride my pony."

"You were a natural, Case," James said. "From the very beginning, you were a natural and you became my able and willing helper when you were barely able to walk."

"No shit?" Case said.

"None whatsoever. When you were seven-years-old you were leading the 'pacas to the shearers, chasing down the ones who had wandered off, and rounding them up. You learned to ride your pony when you were not much older than seven. I used to love watching you run at full speed toward that pony and leap and put your left foot in the stirrup, and swing your right leg over the saddle, then spurring him on at a full gallop after a runaway alpaca. By the age of fourteen, you were my right-hand man and were as capable as any hired-hand I had ever had."

"Well, you taught me how to do all that."

"I know, but you had it in your blood," James said.

Lupita had been a blessing to James MacNicol, as well, since she and her husband, Jose, had first come to work for him. After Jose died, James asked Lupita to stay on. He offered to house her in the second floor of the house. Lupita agreed and moved her belongings in from Boulder. She raised Case from the time he was five, after his parents were killed and, according to her, was still raising him when he was a grown man.

In the early years, Case would call Lupita "Grandma" and she would correct him. "No, Casey," she would tell him. "You had a wonderful grandmother, Miss Amy was your grandmother, *tu abuela*," she taught him in Spanish.

By the time he was in high school, he was skilled in conversational Spanish. Lupita loved the boy like he was her own. It often seemed that she had forgotten that he was not her own child. When she read to him at bedtime, in English at first and in ensuing years in Spanish, his angelic face looked at her adoringly. He clung to her and she to him. Slowly, inevitably, as his relationship with his grandfather and his commitment to the ranch and the business grew, his dependence on Lupita lessened, although his love for her never did. She still catered to him like a guardian angel, and he still treated her like she was his mother or his grandmother.

Case insisted that Lupita not clean his room. "You work hard enough," he told her over and over. "I can make my own bed and wash my clothes. I don't want you working so hard."

"But I don't mind, Casey. It's not too much," she always responded.

And every day when he came in from school, and later from work, he would find his bed made and his clothes washed and dried and neatly folded and put away in his drawers.

It never failed that, when James picked him up from school every afternoon, there were always at least three girls tagging along with him. He'd already figured that the boy was going to be a big hit with members of the opposite sex, but he hadn't expected for the evidence of such to begin at age eleven.

James received a call one afternoon, informing him that Case had been caught in the hall janitor's closet with four girls engaged in a kissing experiment.

In the principal's office, with his amorous grandson, while the four objects of the grandson's affection waited in the outside office, Case was given an opportunity to explain his action in the closet.

"They asked me to kiss them all," he told the principal.

"And what was the reason for their asking you to kiss them all at the same time?"

"They wanted me to be the judge of which one was the best kisser," Case responded.

The principal, a Mister Jamieson, looked at the boy with a mixture of amusement and skepticism. "Case, did you not consider that, if you picked one girl, the others might get their feelings hurt?"

"I wasn't going to pick one girl over any of the others, Mister Jamieson."

"Oh, then what did you intend to do?"

"I was going to kiss them as long as they would let me and then tell them they were all the best."

Jamieson pushed back in his chair and looked at James MacNicol. A slight smile pursed his lips. "The boy is honest, Mister MacNicol. I'll give him that."

"He has no guile in him," James responded, "or he just hasn't learned to lie yet."

"It's relatively harmless now, at this age, but in a few years, well, you see the potential problem," Jamieson said.

"I do," he replied then turned to address his grandson. "Case, son, you can't do this again. You can't be kissing girls in school, at your age. Their parents are not going to be happy about this. One day, you might have a daughter and then you'll understand."

"But they asked me to do it, Grandpa."

"You're not in any trouble, Case," Jamieson told him. "I'm going to have Mrs. Wilson talk to the girls and

I'm sure the girls will confirm your story. I know you didn't force all four of them into that closet."

On the ride home, James looked over at his grandson and started chuckling and shaking his head.

Case looked at him. "What are you laughing at, Grandpa?"

"Damn, son, four at a time? You think maybe that one day you can settle on just one?"

Case just smiled. "I just hated to tell them no, Grandpa."

Case was rounding up some of the animals that had wandered to the farther perimeter of the property. Alpacas were curious and playful creatures and often wandered off like errant teenagers. His cell phone rang. It was Martin Seymour from the BBG.

"Hey, buddy, what's up?" Case answered.

"Case, I just wanted to let you know that this coming Saturday we're having a big entertainment event. Have you heard of the Bobby Billings Band?"

"I've heard the name but that's about it."

"It's an alternative and Indie music band, very popular and very good. Going to be a lot of women here and a lot of fun will be had by all. I just thought you might want to be here."

"I will be there, Martin," Case said. "Thanks for letting me know."

"I'll reserve you a table with Andrea's Angels."

"You're all heart, Martin. You sure you're not trying to get me killed?"

Martin laughed. "No, pal, just giving you some options."

"I'll see you Saturday."

He didn't call Andrea to tell her about the event. He knew he didn't have to. Nothing went on at the BBG that those girls didn't know about. They would be there lined up like queen bees.

The band had started playing when he walked into the dance stage room. Sure enough, the girls were all there at their usual table. Kim spotted him first and yelled at him to come over. He could see that annoyed Andrea but she didn't make a big deal out of it. Andrea had a chair leaned against the table that she had been saving for him. He sat down and ordered a beer when the waitress came over.

"Anybody need anything?" he asked them, pointing his finger around the table, and before anyone could answer he told the waitress to bring another round for everyone. "Put it on my tab," he told her.

At the end of the table was the new girl with the strong handshake. He hadn't expected to see her again. She just didn't seem to be the type that would hang out with Andrea and her gang for very long. He waved to her and she smiled at him and waved back. He stared at her for a moment and she held his gaze. Something about her eyes wouldn't let him go. He had to divert his gaze to respond to someone at the next table, and when he looked back at her, she was still staring at him. He smiled at her again, subtly, and she did as well.

During a break, Case got up to walk around and socialize a bit. He talked to Martin for a few minutes, complimenting him on bringing the talent to the bar. He saw Angie waiting for an order at the bar, and he walked over to her.

"You get better looking every time I see you, Angie."

"Oh, Case, I didn't see you. Lot of good it does me, you never take me out."

"When is your next day off?"

"Are you serious?"

"I think so, let me check," He started patting his chest and his pants pockets like he was looking for something. "Yeah, it looks like I'm serious."

"Oh my," she said, "I'm off this Wednesday."

"How about dinner?"

Angie looked at him wide-eyed. "I'd love that, Case, yes."

"Write your address and phone number down for me and I'll pick you up about six on Wednesday, Okay?"

She wrote down the information on a napkin and handed it to him. He folded it and put it in his wallet. Then he went back to Andrea's table and listened to the band for a while.

He spent the night with Andrea and, as always, she

was mad when he had to leave early for work.

"But I wanted you to take me to breakfast, Case," she cooed.

"Don't you know how to cook?" he asked her as he went out the door.

About eight o'clock on Wednesday night, he and Angie were in the shower at Angie's apartment. When they had dried off he told her, "Get dressed."

"Get dressed, why?" she said.

"I'm taking you to dinner. Remember, I asked you out to dinner."

"You don't have to take me to dinner, Case. I got what I wanted, twice."

"I want to take you to dinner."

"Will you stay the night with me?"

"I can't tonight, Angie. I have an early start in the morning. Maybe next time."

Lighting up with his promise of a "next time," she quickly dressed and did her hair.

"Thank you, Case," she told him, when he brought her back to her apartment. "I wish you could spend the night but I understand about your job. I hope you meant what you said about a next time."

"I did mean it. It was really nice being with you, Angie."

"It was really nice having you with me, Case. Thank you again."

He'd made up his mind that he was going to break it

off with Andrea. The negatives, of having her around were starting to outweigh the positives. He didn't want to hurt her, that could be counterproductive, but it had to be done. He'd hoped that by now she would have had enough of him and would have stormed off and away on her own, but she was not showing any inclination to do that.

He thought about using Angie as a foil but nixed the idea because it might cause her problems with her job. And he didn't want Martin to know that he'd been stiffing one of his employees.

The answer to his problem came in a most surprising way one afternoon at the BBG when Martin asked him to come into his office in the back of the restaurant.

"I want to show you something, Case."

"Okay, what's going on?"

"Remember when we had the Billings band. I shot some video footage to use for an ad campaign I'm going to be doing for the business. Anyway, I concentrated mainly on people dancing and enjoying the band. I got some good footage of Andrea's Angels and you, of course, sitting there watching the band playing."

"They were pretty good, Martin."

"Thanks, but what I have to have is signed waivers from everyone on the video before I can use it for commercial purposes."

"Oh, well my going rate for personal appearances is a thousand bucks."

"Holy shit," Martin said, flabbergasted. "That's a little over my budget."

"Well, in that case, I'll do it for nothing."

Martin let out a sigh of relief. "Aw hell, Case, don't mess with me like that."

"I had you going there for a second."

"You did, but that's not what I wanted you to see. Let me get my laptop fired up." Martin clicked on the video he had taken that night and the camera was panning by the table where Case and all the girls were sitting. "All right," he said, "I panned you guys for quite a while and I didn't notice this until I downloaded the video to my computer. You will note that everyone at the table, including yourself, was watching the band."

"I was watching Angie."

'Oh, so everyone at the table, except you, was watching the band. That Bobby Billings is going to make it big one day, I'd bet on that. But look at the girl on the end. Do you know that girl's name?"

Case peered at the laptop screen. "That's Emily, she's new to their dormitory. She's not watching the band. What is she looking at?"

"She's looking at you."

"Really, you think so?"

"I know so, Case. I watched her during the entire song. She never took her eyes off you."

"I can't help it if I'm good looking, Martin."

"None of us handsome devils can, Case, but that's

not my point. You have to study her demeanor, the look on her face."

"Well, look, pal, I'll concede that you can read people a lot better than I can. Tell me what this means. Does she want to thrill me or kill me?"

"Maybe both before it's all over. But the look on her face is unique. I've watched you interact with the women around here. The ones who take a shine to you, which are most of them here, they always have a sort of desperate and hungry look. But this girl is different. She's not looking at you like she wants your body or like she wants to tame you. It's a different look."

"Well, now, I'm curious. You're the people expert. Tell me what she's thinking, and how I can use it to my advantage."

"I think she's looking at you, trying to figure out who you really are, you know, down deep inside. This girl is smarter than all those other...how shall I put this?"

"Airheads?"

"That's the word," Martin said, pointing both his index fingers at Case. "She's analyzing you. My guess is that she thinks your philandering is all a show, a mask, if you will, a way of covering up what's really inside you."

"That's pretty deep, Martin. Do you think that's really what she's thinking?"

"I do, Case, and wait just a minute. I want you to see when she takes off her glasses. About right here."

In the video, Emily took off her glasses and laid

them down on the table. Then she brushed her hair back off of her face and held it back, apparently trying to cool off a bit.

"Holy shit," Case said.

"That's what I'm talking about. Case, you see that face?"

"My god, Martin, she's beautiful. I never noticed it that much until now. She always has those stupid glasses on and her hair is always covering too much of her face. I knew there was something about her that was drawing me to her but it wasn't her looks. Now I see she comes with a bonus."

"That was exactly what I was thinking. There is something going on between you and that girl, even though neither of you is yet aware of it."

"It's her eyes," Case said.

"Her eyes?"

"Yeah, every time I look in her eyes, I lose my equilibrium and can't think of anything else. It's like they capture me and hold me prisoner. I'm helpless and I do stupid stuff."

"Wow, that sounds like a good country song," Martin said.

"I know, and now I'm going to have to take a closer look at Miss Emily, whatever her last name is. Can you take a screen shot of that clip with her holding her hair back?"

"I can and I will, and I'll email it to you. Are you smitten, Case?"

"I don't know what I'm feeling right now," Case responded. "I've had several 'eye' encounters with her that made me nervous and that never happens."

"Well, I hope you figure it out, pal. You need to be rescued from yourself. Some woman is going cut off your 'thing' one night while you're asleep if you keep on the way you're going now."

"Damn that would hurt. Thanks, Martin, I appreciate this."

Case went to sleep that night thinking about Emily "whatever her last name is." He was not ready for this. His life had suddenly gotten more complicated.

CHAPTER 6

The Dance

Case didn't leave the ranch for two weeks. The work load did not demand it, but he felt the need to immerse himself in his duties. James was pleasantly surprised, for his grandson had suddenly become a dynamo. He was up before dawn every morning and worked late into the evening. When the work played out, he made work and seemed obsessed with staying busy.

"Are you okay, Case?" his grandfather asked.

"Sure, Grandpa, I just decided to try and make up for my screwing off all the time."

"You've been working your ass off, son. There really isn't much left to do. If you keep this up, I'm going to have to let some of the hired hands go, and that wouldn't be fair to them. What's troubling you?"

"I'm not sure just yet but, as soon as I figure it out, I'll come and talk to you about it. Okay?"

"That's fair enough. Let me know if there's anything I can do."

"I will, Grandpa," Case said.

He cleaned up his apartment and repainted the walls. Made some other repairs and bought some new furniture. The place had not been remodeled in years and had not had new furniture ever. He replaced the water heater and bought some new light fixtures.

One of the helpers, a man named Jimmy Gonzales, had done some electrical work so Case asked him about doing some electrical work on the apartment.

"Jimmy, can you replace all the plugs and switches and light fixtures in my apartment?"

"Sure, Case," Jimmy said, "I'll need to get a count but you'll have to pick out some light fixtures. I don't know what kind of fixtures you want."

"Okay, I'll go into town and get the fixtures. If you'll write down how many switches and plugs I need, I'll pick them up too."

Jimmy made a list of the receptacles and switches and wall plates. Case went to a lighting fixture and electrical supply house in Boulder and picked up the materials.

When the work was finished, Case went and got his grandpa and Lupita to come and take a look. James marveled at what Case had done. Lupita smiled at him, then they had a running question and answer session in Spanish. "You have a girlfriend?" she asked.

"No, Lupita."

"Oh yes, my Casey, it's true. You are in love with a woman. I know."

"Okay, my Lupita, maybe it's true but don't tell him I said that, please. I need this to be a secret between you and me for now."

"Of course, no problem."

An email came from Martin. Just as Martin had promised, there was the picture attached that he'd told Case he would send to him. Martin had taken it to a printer and had it done professionally then copied it to his computer.

Case was surprised and elated. He put the picture on his computer as his background wall so he would see it every time he used it. Nobody but Lupita ever came into his apartment so he wasn't worried about someone seeing it and becoming curious. The favor warranted a trip into town to thank Martin for sending the picture.

"Haven't seen you in a while, Case, where you been?"

"We had a busy two weeks, Martin. Those little assholes are like babies. You have to treat them like babies or they start complaining."

"You talking about your alpacas or Andrea's Angels."

Case laughed out loud. "The 'pacas. They're a lot of trouble and work but I love them, I really do. Hey, Martin, you have time for lunch. Let's get something to eat, on me."

They went to a local steak house and ordered T-bones.

"So, what do you plan to do about that girl, Case?"

"I don't know yet," Case said. "I haven't stopped thinking about this for the last two weeks. I got the picture you sent, thanks for that."

"My pleasure," Martin said. "I think you should talk to her about it."

"Well, as strange as this may sound, I'm a little nervous about doing that."

"That's a good sign, my friend," Martin said.

"I'm plotting."

"Don't do that, just let it happen, and it will. She'll be back in the bar with the others and you can just wait for the right moment. If she doesn't come back with them, go to the dorm and find her. One of the girls is getting married next month sometime. I'm sure they'll invite you. She already invited me."

"Please tell me it's Andrea," Case said.

"No, I think Andrea said it's Mara, the redhead."

"She's quite a catch. Who's the lucky guy, do you know?"

"He's not a regular. I've never met him. Do you think Mara will suggest you for the 'best man'?"

Case chuckled "I hope not. Mara is a screamer and a scratcher. I hope she forgets she ever knew me."

Martin chuckled. "Damn, Case, if you ever stop coming into my bar, I won't have any women customers."

"Maybe you should put me on the payroll."

"I'm not sure how I would explain that to corporate."

"It's just as well. I don't like to keep regular hours anyway. Let me ask you a question, Martin. If you think I'm intruding just tell me and I'll shut up."

"You're wondering why my wife is not here with me?"

"That's exactly what I was thinking. I mean, you're a decent looking guy, you have a good job. You're smart as a whip. You have to be a good husband, I would think"

"My wife didn't want to leave her family in Indiana when I was offered the opportunity to come here and manage the BBG. I know that sounds strange but they are a very close nit religious family."

"She hasn't asked for a divorce?" Case asked him.

"No, not so far. I've expected it but she says she still loves me. I keep telling her how great it is out here but her folks have very strong hold on her."

"What's her name?"

"Victoria, but her family calls her Vicky. I prefer Victoria, sounds classier I think, but they call her Vicky."

"Do you have a picture of her?" Case said.

Martin reached for his phone, pulled up a photo, and handed Case the phone.

"She's very attractive, buddy. You better go get her."

"Do you think I should give her an ultimatum? You know, decide if she wants to be a wife or a daughter."

"I don't know. I think eventually you will have to be prepared to do that. I mean, how long can you go on like this?"

"I guess I'm just afraid of what her response will be."

"That's a damned shame, Martin. I was just curious. I knew you weren't gay and I never see you try and hit on any women in the bar."

"I won't cheat on my wife unless and until we get a divorce."

"Then it wouldn't be cheating," Case said.

"Good point."

"Is there anything I can do, you know, write her a letter and tell what a great man her husband is?"

"Nah, but I appreciate your concern. She's going to have to work it out herself. Anyway, thanks for lunch, Case. Oh, and how did you know I'm not gay?"

"You never tried anything with me."

"You're not my type, too domineering. You'd want to get on top."

"Now that hurts my feelings, Martin," Case said. "I thought we were closer than that."

They left the restaurant, laughing. Case received a call from Mara confirming that she was indeed getting married. "Who is the lucky guy, Mara?"

"It's a guy I met in Denver. His name is Jeremy, he's a lawyer, a wonderful man."

"I'm happy for you and I appreciate the invitation. I will certainly be there."

"Thank you, Case, I was so hoping you would come to my wedding. It means a lot to me."

"I don't know why it would but I'll be there, just the same."

"You know why, but that's in the past. I know that you will never marry me, and Jeremy asked me so I said yes."

"I'll be on my best behavior, Mara, I promise."

"You are always on your best behavior, Case."

"Will your whole gang be there?"

"Yes, all my friends. Emily Quarters, the bookworm, and I have become pretty good friends. I'm bringing her with me. If you can give her a ride home, you'd be doing me a favor."

"As long as she doesn't talk as much as you do, I think I can handle that."

"Just don't you hit on her. She's not like the rest of us. She's quieter and more serious."

"I think she has a thing for me, Mara."

"Oh, Case, you think every woman has a thing for you."

"Most of them do."

"Emily is different. You better not try anything with her, I mean it."

"I'll be a gentleman, Mara, I promise," he said.

Lupita was cleaning Case's room, like she always did, despite his insistence that she let him do it. He had forgotten to turn off his computer and, when she moved it to dust off his desk, the screen lit up. Emily's picture popped up on the screen and Lupita giggled like a schoolgirl. "My Casey, he has a girlfriend and such a beautiful girl." She wanted to run and tell James but she remembered that she and Case had an agreement not to tell his grandfather anything that confirmed what he had told her about having a lady friend.

The wedding was not held in a church but rather in a huge estate on Evergreen Lake in Evergreen. The nuptials took place in the same room in which the reception was taking place.

After the proverbial knot was tied, there was the typical seemingly never-ending parade of one tuxedoed nerd after another, toasting the bride and groom. They were all Jeremy's friends.

Andrea managed to get though a slurred speech soliloquy in honor of her "best friend" Mara and about what a wonderful couple she and Jeremy would make.

Case looked around at the house and the palatial surroundings. He leaned over to Martin and whispered. "Mara must have ripped ol' Jeremy's back to shreds and broken all their fine china with her screaming, to land this rich shmuck."

"Don't get me to laughing, Case, please," Martin replied, covering his mouth so no one could see him chuckling."

The band started playing. Jeremy and Mara had their dance then announced that everyone else was free to "dance their asses off."

Case looked around for Andrea's gang and they were all sitting at one large table not too far from where he and Martin were sitting. Emily was in a chair next to Josie. "Wish me luck, buddy, I'm going to break some new ground. I may be back here in a minute with my tail tucked between my legs."

"Go for it, Case. The worst she can do is laugh at you."

"Thanks for the encouragement," Case said sheepishly.

He started walking toward the table, suddenly got cold feet, and started to turn around. *Oh shit*, he was thinking, *what is happening to me? I haven't been so nervous to approach a girl since Junior High.* Some of the girls at the table saw him walking their way, and they assumed he was going to ask Andrea to dance, but Andrea was off somewhere else in the building.

He managed to find his courage and kept on walking toward the table and toward what would either be embarrassment for him or the beginning of a whole new chapter in his life. What would he do if she told him no? No girl ever had before but might karma come in the form of a beautiful brown-haired girl he didn't even know yet. "Fuck it," he said out loud, to no one in particular. "The worst thing that can happen is I'll be humiliated."

When he was just a few feet from their table, every girl at that table started looking at him trying to figure out what his intentions were. No one spoke and it was as if the world had stopped to wait for this scene to play out. There was no chair next to Emily so he knelt down on one knee beside her.

She looked at him, stunned, wondering what in the world he was going to do.

He just stared at her for a few seconds and she stared back at him. Then he found his voice.

"Emily, will you dance with me?"

She was stunned but managed not to show it. "Are you serious?" she asked him.

"My god," Josie yelled out. "I think Case is proposing to Emily."

Everyone looked at her but no one commented on her proclamation.

"Yes, Emily, I am serious," he said.

"Well, of course, I'd love to dance with you, Case."

He took her hand and led her to the dance floor just as the music was starting. He held her arm up and twirled her around, pulling her into his arms as she completed the turn.

"I was afraid you might say no."

"What would you have done if I had?"

"I would have poured your drink in your lap and walked out the door."

"Oh, you would not," she said, laughing.

"Honestly I hadn't thought that far ahead."

"Why *did* you ask me to dance, Case?"

"When we get to know each other better, I'll tell you why."

"Are we going to get to know each other better?"

"I sure hope so because I've been fretting over this for at least a month now."

"Well, I hope you had a good reason because your girlfriend is shooting daggers at me with her eyes right now."

He turned her around. "There, now you can't see her, and she's not my girlfriend."

"I don't think she knows that."

"Do you have any plans for tonight, Emily?"

She looked as if she had just had a cruel joke played on her. "I'm not going to bed with you, Case. If that's what this is all about, we might as well end it right now."

"No, no, Emily, it's not. I promise you it's not. I want to take you to dinner. Will you have dinner with me tonight?"

"Yes," she said, relieved. "I'd like that, really, but this is strange for me. You have to understand why I would be confused about all this."

"You can't be any more confused about it than I am."

"Now, I really don't understand that. You asked me to dance, and you don't know why?"

"Well, I know why I did it but I just can't tell you right now. What time is it?" He looked at his watch. "It's four o'clock. Let's go now, Emily. Can we leave now? There's something I want to show you before we go to dinner."

Still confused but thrilled by the sudden attention she was receiving from this handsome, mysterious man, she nodded. "I'll get my purse." She started walking back to the table where the other girls were waiting with slack jaws. Andrea had already stormed out of the place.

"What's going on, Emily?" Lana asked her."

"I don't know. He wants to take me to dinner, and there's something he wants to show me first. I'm as confused as you are."

Before they left, Case found the keeper of the gift basket for the newlyweds and dropped an envelope in it. Then they walked out to his truck. He opened the door for her and helped her in. She remained confused and a bit apprehensive all the way back to Boulder. But when he headed out Boulder Canyon Road, she was even more dumbfounded.

"Where in the world are we going, Case?"

"Just sit tight, I'll show you."

"How does one sit 'tight'?" she asked him.

"It's just and expression. Hold on, we're almost there."

He drove about five miles out of boulder and slowed as they passed a sign that said *Magnolia Road* with an arrow that pointed left. He turned onto Highway 132, which was the road the sign had directed them to. It was almost a U-turn and he swung around sharply sliding her against the door. In a short time, he turned in at a sign that read, *Magnolia Road Ranch.*

Emily's head was spinning now. She remembered the other girls saying that Case never took anyone to his ranch and here she was riding with him onto his ranch.

"This is your ranch, Case?"

"Mine and my grandfather's," he said. He honked the horn at two very wooly, white dogs to keep them away from the truck.

"My gosh, what beautiful dogs. They're Great Pyrenees, aren't they?"

"Yes, they're my Grandpa's dogs, Bogie and Bacall."

Emily started laughing. "Bogie and Bacall?"

"My grandpa is kind of eccentric but they are really good guard dogs, they're very protective of the animals."

He got out, went around, opened the door for her, and took her hand to help her out of the truck. He led her into the alpaca barn to a stall on the end that was distinctly separate from the rest of the herd and showed her Rudy. "This is Rudy, my prize winner. He's won top prize in the Colorado competition for the last two years."

"Oh my gosh, he's darling, he's beautiful. Can I pet him?"

"Of course, he loves the attention."

"He's so soft, Case, like a big stuffed animal. So, this is what you do, raise prize alpacas?"

"Rudy is sort of a hobby. We raise the alpacas for their wool and for breeding. We sell them to people either for pets or to start their own business."

"It's beautiful out here. I love that the mountains are so close to you."

"Next time you're here, we'll take a horseback trip up that close one there." He pointed to the one he used to ride up when he was a boy.

"I look forward to that, except I've never ridden a horse."

"I'll teach you how. It's not hard. The horse does all the work, all you have to do is not fall off. I want you to meet my grandpa if he's around. Come on, let's go the house. Be really quiet, he's got a lot of guns in the house," Case said, and the look on Emily's face made him bust out laughing. "I was joking, Emily, I was just trying to get a rise out of you."

"I was hoping you were but this 'is' our first date, after all."

He opened the door and called out, "Grandpa!"

"Come on in, Case," James answered from inside.

"I have someone here I want you to meet, Grandpa."

James got up from his chair and approached them. "Who's this?"

"This is Emily Quarters, Grandpa, a friend of mine who goes to CU."

Emily watched the older man, silver hair and tanned skin that looked as tough as leather. He was about the same height as Case and was still a handsome man, even at his age. She could venture a guess as to his age but he moved around with at least as much ease as her own dad, and he was fifty-seven. She quickly surmised that James MacNicol was probably around sixty-four, but he looked ten years younger. She guessed that he probably looked like Case when he was the same age.

"Well, hello, miss. I'm happy to meet you. Case never brings any females home to meet me. I think he's afraid I'll flirt with them."

"I'm happy to meet you too, Mister MacNicol," Emily said and held out her hand.

James shook it. "You have a strong handshake for a young lady, Emily."

"That's what Case says," she said, looking over at Case.

Lupita came into the room, immediately got excited, and started talking to Case in Spanish. "Oh Casey, she's the girl in the picture on your computer."

"Ai yi, yi, Lupita, don't tell anyone, remember our secret," Case said, trying to shush her.

"Oh, I'm sorry," Lupita said, putting both hands over her mouth. "Will you eat with us?"

"We're going out to dinner tonight, Lupita. Can I bring her back another time for dinner?"

"Sure, sure, any night, just tell me before and I make a good meal."

"Thank you, I'll let you know in plenty of time."

They talked to James for about a half hour until Case said, "Emily looks hungry, Grandpa. I think we better get on back to town."

"I'm betting that you are the one that's hungry," James replied. "But go on and get this young lady something good to eat."

After they left the ranch, Emily turned her back to the door of the truck and leaned back, she sat there staring at Case until he got nervous.

"What?" he said.

"What's going on here, Case?"

"What do you mean?"

"Lupita said something to you that you didn't want me to know. Will you tell me what it was?"

"You don't speak Spanish, do you?"

"No, I speak French and I could make out a little of what she said, but it was your reaction to what she was saying that made me curious. She was saying something you didn't want me to know."

"I'm going to ask you to trust me for a while. I can't tell you right now, but I will."

"When we get to know each other better."

He looked at her and nodded his head.

"Okay, Case MacNicol. You're being very strange, but today you've made me feel like a million bucks. So, I'll trust you until you're ready to tell me why, all of a sudden, I am getting so much attention from you."

He took her back to the dorm after dinner. He didn't try to kiss her, although she looked as if she was expecting it. He kissed her hand, and, later, he wished that he had kissed her, but there would always be a next time.

The girls pounced on her, like vultures waiting for something to die.

They insisted on hearing all the details.

"Did you go to bed with him?" Kim asked her.

"We went to dinner after we went to his ranch."

"Oh my god, you went to his ranch, what did you do there?"

She related the entire story to them, meeting Rudy, the prize-winning alpaca, meeting the grandfather and the housekeeper, Bogie and Bacall, the dogs. She was going back to the ranch for dinner later in the week.

"Then he brought me home. He didn't even kiss me. Frankly I was a little disappointed about that. He did kiss my hand, which I thought was very sweet."

"What in the world is going on in that man's mind? Has he gone insane?"

"You don't see what's going on here?" Josie demanded, joining in the conversation.

"What are you talking about, Josie? Lana asked.

"Case is in love with Emily."

"Oh, come on, you can't be serious," Kim said, and they all turned and looked at Emily.

"Don't look at Emily," Josie said. "She's love-struck. Think about it. This man has never taken any woman to his ranch and he dances with Emily one time and it's home to meet the family, kisses her hand when he brings her home. If that's not love, I don't know what you'd call it because it's not like anything the man has ever done before."

Emily shrugged her shoulders. "I don't know," she said. "He was acting strangely, that's all I know. I have to go to bed and try to process this."

The next morning at the ranch, Case went to the house to talk to his grandfather. "Grandpa," he said, "how did you get so smart?"

James smiled broadly. "You're in love with that girl, aren't you, son?"

"I don't know, Grandpa. I think so, I may be. Yes, I'm in love with her. I've never been in love before. I don't know how to act."

"You got a good start, bringing her home to meet your family. Are you going to tell her?"

"I'm going to have to tell her pretty soon or else I'll lose my mind."

"She looks like a perfect match for you, Case. You need to tell her how you feel."

"I will, Grandpa. I just have to work up the nerve to do it."

They both laughed at that.

A few days later Case brought Emily to the ranch for dinner. Lupita had given him a long list of groceries and other items she needed to make a special dinner for Emily. She made roast beef, mashed potatoes, and several other vegetables. During dinner, Emily told them about her plan to get her degree and to work with special needs children.

"You must be a brain," James told her.

"I've had to work very hard," Emily replied.

"I'm so glad you brought your girl to dinner, Case. I hope you enjoyed it, Miss Emily."

"Everything was delicious, Lupita. I really enjoyed it. Let me help you with the dishes."

"No, no, you go on with Casey. He wants to tell you how much he loves you."

"Oh, hell, Lupita—I'm sorry, but you weren't supposed to say that. I thought we had a deal."

"She's a beautiful girl, and so smart. Go ahead, tell her you love her."

"Let's go for a walk," he said and reached for Emily's hand."

"But I need to help with the dishes."

Lupita waved her arms at Emily. "No, no, you go ahead, I do the dishes."

"So, you love me?" Emily said after they were out-side.

"Believe me. I'm as surprised as you are."

"But how could this happen, Case? You barely know me."

"I know, everything that's happened to me in the past month is totally illogical. Let me tell you how this started." They sat down on a bench in the back yard and he began telling her about Martin's video. He told her about the picture and how his feelings for her had hit him like a ton of bricks. "I don't know exactly how it happened, Emily, I just know it did. You know how I got all bumfuddled just looking into your eyes."

"Really? I thought that was all just an act."

"Hmm, not hardly, I have a picture of you on my desktop screen that Martin sent me off the video. It's not just because you're beautiful. There is much more to it than that. I started to realize that you were nothing at all like any of the girls I have ever known. And that is what I have been needing and searching for all my adult life."

"And you learned this from bedding half the women in Colorado."

"Just in Boulder County."

"Sorry, half the women in Boulder County?"

"It wasn't anywhere near half, Emily. And that doesn't matter anymore, anyway."

"Well, it might matter to me, Case. Did you consider that?"

"I did and I know I have an uphill battle to prove myself worthy of you. All the talking in the world won't convince you that I have suddenly changed, but if you'll give me time, I will show you that I am sincere."

"I want to see the picture," she said.

"Okay, it's in my apartment." He took her there.

"This is a really nice place. It's kind of like a garage apartment, only it's a barn apartment. I am impressed. I honestly wasn't expecting it to look livable."

"After I decided to ask you out, I spent two weeks remodeling this place. I painted the walls, got all new furniture and light fixtures, just in case I ever got you in here."

"It's really nice, Case, and I see my picture on your screen. I'm a little overwhelmed. I've never had a guy show me this much attention. I guess you'd better kiss me if we're going to get this thing started."

He pulled her to him, their lips met, and they spent a mad minute of passion before they pulled apart. Both were breathing heavily. "Wow," she said. "I've never been kissed like that."

"Neither have I," he told her. "Come on, let's get away from this bed, it's making me nervous." He took her back outside. "I want to know all about you. I don't even know where you're from."

"I'm from Vermont."

"Vermont?" He pondered that for a moment. "So that's why you talk funny?"

"You think I talk funny?"

"Well, you called my apartment a gairege apairt-ment."

"Yes, Case," she said, laughing. "That's why I talk funny. It's my Vermont accent."

"I may have to get a Vermont to English dictionary."

"I'll try to learn your language, senor."

"No, don't you change a thing. I like you just the way you are."

"I can do that too. So, what do you want to know about me?"

"I want to know why you came to Colorado, what you're doing at school, and where you plan to do your work with children after you graduate. I want to know everything about you. I need you to help me understand why I fell in love with you."

"Well then, we'd better go back and sit down on that bench," she said. She told him about her family and about her brother and how she had taught him to deal with his autism. She told him about the school in Burlington that had sponsored her to come to CU and about her commit-ment to go back and work for them for a number of years, in their special needs program.

"That's why then. I knew there was more to you than just a pretty face and a great body. I guess I'm not as su-perficial as people think I am. I saw that in you before I really knew you. So, I guess my question is, Emily Quar-ters, will you go steady with me?"

"Oh, gosh," she said, giggling. "I haven't gone steady since high school and even then, it wasn't all that steady."

"Neither have I but I want to go steady with you now."

"Okay, my beautiful man, we are officially going steady. You may kiss me again now." And he did. After a few minutes, she asked him, "When we make love, and I think we both know we will eventually, what number will I be?"

"What do you mean?" he said quizzically.

"I mean you have a lot of notches on your bedpost and broken hearts spread all over Boulder County." He rolled his eyes at that. "Which one will I be—number ten, fifteen, twenty, what number will I be?"

"You'll be the last one, Emily. The very last one. I promise you that."

The next week, Emily went to a hairdresser and had her bangs cut back and her hair styled to part down the middle so that it would fall away from her face and over her ears. She began using hair clips to hold her hair back farther off her face and started curling it in ringlets on the sides. It was vanity, she admitted, but she didn't do it to catch a man, she did it to please the man she already had. She immediately began drawing attention and compliments from men and women alike.

"Now the world is starting to see what I already knew all along," Case said. "And it was your inner beauty that had attracted me to you, not the fact that you were drop-dead gorgeous."

Case took a chance that Andrea would be at her apartment and went there to offer an explanation for what he was certain she must surely consider a betrayal on his part. She answered the door, immediately grew angry, and lashed out at him.

"What the hell do you want?" she screamed.

"I need to talk to you, Andrea. I know you're hurt."

"I'm not hurt, I'm pissed."

"That's good, that's a good thing, turn it into anger. You can get through anything if you get mad enough. Listen, Andrea. I'm really sorry. The last thing I meant to do was hurt your feelings. I hope you can forgive me. I don't want to go on, thinking you hate me."

"I don't hate you, Case, I love you," she said, suddenly starting to cry. "Why did you do this to me?"

"Things happen, Andrea. I'll be honest with you. I fell in love. I don't know how it happened, I don't know exactly when it happened. I just know I fell in love with Emily, and it's changed my life. I didn't mean to hurt you, and I wanted to come and apologize and explain it to you."

"Will you kiss me?" she asked him.

"I can't, Andrea. I can't ever kiss another woman but her again. I hope you understand. You're a beautiful woman. You will meet and marry someone, and you'll be happy. You always told me you wanted to go back to

Virginia. And you knew I would never leave Colorado. Just tell me you'll forgive me. It would mean a lot to me."

"I'll never be able to hate you, Case," she said. "But it hurt so much to see you with her. I knew something was up that night you gave her a ride to the dorm and walked her to the door. That really hurt me."

"I know it did, and I didn't plan it like it happened," he lied, "but it hit me like a ton of bricks and now a life with Emily is the only thing I can ever imagine."

He hugged her, quickly letting go of her, and left before her mood could change again.

That went better than I expected, he was thinking, as he drove away from her apartment and headed back to the ranch.

CHAPTER 7

Shearing

Case was up early and at the back door of the house, announcing his entry so he wouldn't take his grandfather by surprise.

The older MacNicol man was getting on in age and had become more skittish and less tolerant of surprises and loud interruptions. The old man's eyesight was still good, and Case was not as worried about being shot by the snub-nosed .38 revolver his grandfather always carried, as he was of startling him and causing him to become alarmed.

"Grandpa," he called out loudly. "I'm coming in."

"I heard you come up on the porch, Case. You don't have to creep around like a bill collector."

Case laughed at his grandfather's gruffness. "I just didn't want to alarm you, Grandpa."

"That's okay, son, what's up?

"I'm going into town to pick up Emily before the shearing crew gets here. I promised her I'd bring her out for the event."

"Okay, but hurry, they'll be here by eight," his grandfather said.

Case quickly drove the nine miles into Boulder to the dormitory. Emily was standing at the curb waiting for him when he arrived. He came to a stop, jumped out of the truck, and ran around to open the door for her. "Hi, baby," he told her, "you look nice this morning."

"Thanks, handsome," she replied. "I told you I'd be ready, didn't I?"

"You did but I didn't believe you could get up this early on a Saturday morning."

"I told you I would."

"Thank you," he said, "by the way, you're beautiful."

"Thank you, so are you."

He shook his head.

"What?" she asked him.

"I'll never understand how women can say a man is beautiful. I just don't see it."

"That's because you look through a man's eyes. You never will see it until you can see through a woman's eyes."

"Then I suppose I'll have to take your word for it," he said.

She started giggling.

He reached up, turned the rearview mirror toward himself, and looked at his face. "You, beautiful man, you," he said, and she continued laughing.

The ranch consisted of a main residence, which was a typical Colorado two-story wood-frame home with an unfinished basement. Case's grandfather lived on the first floor and the second floor was for the exclusive use of his live-in housekeeper, Lupita. Lupita, despite her name, was not a small woman. She was almost as round as she was tall, but she worked hard, keeping the house immaculately clean, cooking the senior MacNicol's meals, and making sure he took his medicine. She was fiercely loyal to the old man, having worked for him since Case was a young boy.

The barn was about a hundred yards from the house, and it contained stalls for the horses and a mechanic shop for the maintenance of the company vehicles. Equipment, grain, and alfalfa for feeding the animals was also kept in the barn.

A longer barn, almost 300 feet long, doubled as a shearing barn and as winter quarters for the animals. Beyond the long barn was a huge fenced-in pen with a sand bottom for the Alpacas to roll in.

Case and Emily approached the shearing barn. Half its length was divided into individual stables with posts to which each animal could be harnessed while it was being sheared.

"We use a team of professionals to do the shearing," he was explaining to Emily. "The Matthews are a husband, wife, and son family business, and we contract with them to come in at the beginning of every spring. They do the shearing, bag and weigh the wool for us. We could do it in house and save some money but Grandpa can't do it anymore because of his hands and bad knees, and I'm just not very good at it. The noise scares the animals some of the time and they give them a mild sedative."

"How long does it take to do one animal?" she asked him.

"A good tradesman can do one complete in about ten or fifteen minutes or maybe a little less, and these guys are good. It takes me about a week." She started giggling at him and smiled broadly, "Three days if I get a good night sleep before," he said

"How many of them do you have?"

"About a hundred," he said. "We have seventy-five of the standard whites and about twenty-five of the various colors, cinnamon, and that sort. You want to help me bring them to the stables?"

"Of course," she said, "just show me what to do."

"Follow me." He grabbed a couple of harnesses and started toward the holding pen on the other side of the shearing barn, and she walked along with him. He attached the harnesses to two of the alpacas and led them out through the gate. "Which one do you want?"

"This one is cute," she said, pointing at one of them.

He handed the reins to her and took hold of the other one.

"Just be firm, not rough but firm," he told her.

"He doesn't seem to want to come with me."

"Relax a bit then give him a little tug."

"I don't think he likes girls," she said.

"They don't see a lot of women, except curious people who stop on the road to take pictures. Just give him a little tug."

She jerked the reins slightly and the animal bolted and started pulling her the other way. "Oh, oh, Case, what do I do now? He's going the other way."

"Hold him, baby, let him know who's boss," Case yelled to her.

"I think he already knows," she yelled back as the animal turned and started pulling her toward the water tank on the other end of the holding pen. Soon, she was in full stride, unable to release the reins, and still trying to get control of the errant alpaca. She continued yelling as Case ran after them as fast as he could.

"Let go of him," he yelled. "Let go of him, Emily."

But it was too late. The animal had pulled her into the tank and she fell flat on her face in the mud at the edge.

When Case got to her she was crying and laughing at the same time. He couldn't help but laugh as he stood there watching her wallow around in the water and mud. Her clothes were caked with mud and other mysterious matter, the substance of which Case did not want to make her aware.

"I'm sorry," she said, through her tears.

"Aw, come on, honey, it's no big deal," he said. "The very same thing happened to me the first time I started working on the ranch, course I was only seven years old." She started bawling then so he took her under her arms and picked her up. "Don't feel bad, Em. You didn't hurt yourself, did you?"

"No, I don't think so, just my feelings. But what about my clothes?"

"Come on, I've got some extra clothes you can wear, and I'll toss your clothes in the washer." At the apartment, he picked out a pair of Levis and a T-shirt for her. "You can take a shower if you want to but you're going to get hot and sweaty again so why don't you wait until we're through?"

"Okay," she said. She had to roll the pants legs up several turns but she made it work.

"I'll come back in a little while and put your things in the dryer."

They walked back to the herd, and she wanted to pet the alpacas. "They're precious little creatures, almost like fluffy dogs. Tell me more about them, Case. I really want to know more about what you do."

"My grandfather bought this property in 1982 for the

specific purpose of starting an alpaca ranch. Grandpa was a frugal man, still is. He'd worked at various jobs and saved his money. My father was an investment banker so he invested Grandpa's money for him and he did very well, according to what I've been told. It was tough going at first and Casey, that's my father, joined him in the business and they made it work. But there was always a cash flow crisis in the beginning, Grandpa told me. After my parents were killed, he worked his butt off seventy and eighty hours a week for a year or so until he was on his feet. It was worth it, he said, because alpacas are an excellent investment. The wool is comparable to cashmere and is much desired because of its light weight and appearance. The products created from the wool are soft and warm and comfortable. You'll find out because I'm going to have a sweater made for you after this shearing."

"Oh, that will be nice, Thank you, Case."

"You can pick one out, if you like, for your own personal pet. They make good pets. We sell a lot of them to people for pets. They're just a little more expensive than going to the pound and getting a mutt."

"How much does one cost for a pet?" Emily asked.

"About five-hundred to a thousand bucks for a standard 'paca," Case said. "A colored one might go for two grand or more. I wouldn't sell Rudy for less than four grand. Some people come by just to have their kid's pictures taken on one of them."

"Can a child ride on their back?"

"A small child can ride on one and you could use one to carry a light load on a camping trip but they are not big enough to really use for a pack animal. They're very friendly little creatures and fun to watch. They're very gentle with children."

"What's the difference between an alpaca and a llama?"

"They're closely related. Both are from a group of four species known as South American camelids. Llamas are approximately twice the size of an alpaca and are principally used as pack animals. Alpacas are exclusively bred as fleece animals. Most alpacas make very good pets if they are treated well and if owners have realistic expectations. You must keep in mind, they are not dogs. They generally don't like being held and are particularly sensitive to being touched on the head. I think what happened, with the one that dragged you into the water tank, is that you tried to pet him and you spooked him."

"I did," Emily said. "He was just so cute. I wanted to make friends with him."

"That's okay, baby. It's a common mistake people make. Alpacas are naturally curious, and very intelligent and, if you let them approach you, rather than rush at them, then they will be much more affectionate."

"Well, thank you for the seminar on alpacas. I feel almost like an expert now."

"It was my pleasure. This is probably to only thing in the world that I know more about than you do."

"Oh, I don't know about that, my darling. You continue to amaze me, every day, with things I didn't know you knew. I'm curious, though, why didn't you go to CU? You could have lived at home and gotten a degree with relative ease. You are a lot smarter than you let on."

"Grandpa wanted me to do that very thing but I just didn't want to. I have the totality of man's knowledge at my fingertips. I can go to my computer and learn anything I need to know. I have a much better education than I would have gotten at college," he said.

"Because you would not have had to study a lot of useless stuff you didn't need?"

"Exactly, I just study what I need and want to learn. The only thing the internet couldn't teach me was how to fall in love and you came along and showed me how to do that."

"It didn't teach you how to sweep a girl off her feet either, did it?"

"Yes, Bullshit One-Oh-One. I got an A."

"You're incorrigible," Emily said.

"Oh, but you're making me corrigible."

"I don't think that's a word."

"It is now," he said, and she laughed.

Back at the stables, the shearing work was going on unimpeded. "Now watch how they do this, Em. The optimum result is to get as much of the wool off in one piece as possible. It's worth more if you have fewer pieces. Then they bag it, weigh it, and document the quantities. I take it all to a processor, called a spinner, in Denver. They turn it into yarn so it can be made into stuff. We keep a lot of it ourselves and give it to a retail outlet that makes stuff out of it, hats and scarves and stuff like that. We market it under our own brand name called Magnolia Road."

"The road the ranch is on, that's pretty cool," she said.

"That was my idea."

"So, you're a marketing genius."

"Not bad for a bow-legged Mountain William, huh?

"Mountain William?" she said, looking perplexed.

"That's a Colorado hillbilly."

"Oh, you're no hillbilly, Case MacNicol. You're as refined as they come, and you're not bow-legged either."

"Well, I may be considered a bit refined for the environment but I was reaching way out of my class the first time I went over and asked you to dance with me. I mean I was aiming at the moon."

She just stared at him incredulously. "Even in Vermont, we call that bullshit, Case. I almost peed in my pants when you started walking toward me that night. I thought you were headed for one of the other girls, they all did too, but when you knelt down next to me, I didn't know whether to—"

"Shit or go blind."

"If that's means pass out, then yes, I didn't know whether to shit or go blind."

Later, at the main house, Lupita fixed dinner for them and they all ate and talked around the table Lupita and Case spoke a while in Spanish which annoyed his grandfather to no end.

"Why don't you two speak English?" he would say from time to time.

"I'm sorry, Grandfather," Case would tell him in Spanish, "I don't speak English."

And Lupita would giggle and cover her mouth as if the old man could not hear her.

"Don't tell me you don't hablo English. Both of you hablo better English than I do."

Emily loved the banter that went on between the old man and his grandson. James was given to profanity but he did his best to refrain from it when Emily was around, and she liked that. It was clear, to even the most casual observer, that there was very close bond between the two men.

The family dynamic in the MacNicol home was much different from that in which she grew up. Her parents were caring people but there was never a lot of fun around their house. She realized that her brother Murphy's autism caused their entire lives to take on a dire and more serious view of the world.

The MacNicols were hard working men who had suffered greater tragedy in their lives and yet they had not let it ruin their positivity nor their optimism and their lust for life.

Lupita finished the dishes and went upstairs to go to bed. Case hugged his grandfather and then took Emily's hand. "You ready to go, baby?"

"Did you remember to put my clothes in the dryer?"

"No, but I'll do it now," he said.

They walked to the barn where his apartment was and he took her clothes out of the washer and put them in the dryer. "I guess you'll have to stay the night. These mountain roads can get pretty treacherous. I wouldn't want to risk driving you into town at this late hour."

"It's August, Case."

"Oh, right. Well, okay, I'll take you home as soon as your clothes are dry."

"It's such a nice drive. I've never been on Magnolia Road at night. I'm looking forward to it. And I do have some studying I need to catch up on."

"So regular school starts up next week?" he asked.

"Yes, but it seems like I haven't had a break at all."

"You went home in June. I bet your folks were glad to see you, weren't they?"

"They were, but they wanted me to stay all summer. I told them I needed to take the extra classes. That wasn't entirely true, though. Mostly I wanted to get back to you."

"That was a hard month for me, Em. Every night I went to bed I imagined that you wouldn't come back. Luckily, my grandpa worked me hard all month so that helped take my mind off of you for a while, at least until sundown."

She smiled at him. "You don't know how that makes me feel. I went through the same thing, missing you. You know I will graduate this coming May?"

I've thought of nothing but that since I first met you. Are you still planning to go back to Vermont?"

"I don't know. My commitment is there but my heart is here. I have worked toward this goal for four years, and people are counting on me."

"I admire that, Emily, I really do. What you set your sights on doing, you then actually do it. That shows dedication and courage that most people just don't have. But I just can't imagine my life without you."

"I know," she said. The pain in her face only made the pain in his heart just that much worse. She sighed. "I'm so torn between the world I wanted, and pledged myself to, and the world I love and need."

He took her hand. "Come on, let's take a walk. I need to talk to you and tell you something." He led her around behind the barn and out toward the south side of the property.

She stopped suddenly. "Oh my God, Case, you're going to break up with me, aren't you?" she said and was about to start crying.

"What, what did you say?

"You're breaking up with me so I won't feel bad about going back to Vermont."

"No," he said, turning to face her. "Emily, I'm in love with you. I loved you the first time we danced. I think I fell in love with you when we first shook hands that time at the BBG. I'll always love you. I don't want you to go to Vermont, I 'want' you to stay here with me, but I understand that's what you have to do. I want to marry you some day if you'll have me."

"Oh, God, I don't know what to do? Of course, I'll have you. That was a foolish thing to say."

"Can we just put this on hold for now?" he said. "We have time to figure things out. Don't fret about it, or it will interfere with your studies. Let's get some sleep. We have a long day tomorrow. I'll take you home. Remember now, don't take any alpacas on a walk to the water tank."

"Don't worry, I won't." she said, laughing but the issue was still in her mind and she knew she would have to face it sooner or later.

CHAPTER 8

Parting

Snow came fairly early in the winter of 2014. Case MacNicol was a young man in love for the first time in his life, and he wanted to start living life to the fullest.

Despite being a Colorado native and spending most of his life in the mountains, Case didn't know how to ski. Actually, he didn't know how to ski very well. He'd been skiing a number of times but had usually spent more time with his face in the snow than he had with his feet on it. He decided he wanted to take Emily skiing.

"I assume that you know how to ski since you grew up in Vermont. Am I right?" he asked her.

"You are correct, sir, and I am pretty darn good at it," she replied.

"Good, because you may have to hold me up."

"You're telling me you can't ski and you grew up in Colorado?"

"Let's just say I'm no 'Chapstick Chaffee' but I can navigate Bunny Hill with quite a bit of expertise."

"What a name dropper you are. I think you're trying to impress me by mentioning the best female skier of all time. How do you know about Suzy Chaffee?"

"I Googled it before I came to pick you up," he said.

"I should have known. So where are we going?"

"Winter Park, it's not far from here, maybe an hour or so."

"Are we staying overnight?" she said, looking at him mischievously.

"Do you want to stay overnight?"

"Yes," she said. "I brought a change of clothes."

"Okay, then slide over here next to me, baby."

She slid across the seat, snuggled up to him, and put her head on his shoulder.

While Emily skied circles around him, Case measured success by how long he could stay on his feet. They finally were able to make it down a run, as long as she held on to him. Some other skiers nearby remarked that they could certainly tell that Emily was a native of Colorado. "Where is your boyfriend from, Texas?" one woman asked, shaking her head.

"No, he's from Boulder. I'm the one from out of state."

"Oh my," the lady said. You'd think he would have learned how to ski by now. Where are you from, dear?"

"I'm from Vermont. I've been skiing all my life," Emily said. "My boyfriend has other skills that make up for his inability to ski."

"Yes, I expect he does," the lady said, looking at Case approvingly.

Case stumbled over to where Emily was talking to the lady. "You look pretty worn out, Em. You want to take a rest?"

"Yeah, I'm about tuckered out, maybe we should go to the room."

"I made reservations at the Best Western."

After they had settled in, she turned to him. "I have to be honest with you. As much as I wanted to assure myself that you were sincere about your feelings toward me, I was just a wee bit disappointed that you didn't try to get me in bed."

"I apologize for that, baby. It's a mistake I won't make again."

She came to him and he took her in his arms. They kissed like they were starving for each other's lips.

"I had such high expectations of you. The girls in the dorm who knew you, and I mean 'knew' in the biblical term, they convinced me that you were the best lover they had ever been with."

"Oh, don't believe everything you hear from that bunch of airheads," he told her.

"You're telling me it isn't true?"

"No, I'm telling you to determine that for yourself. You make me prove it."

The first time can sometimes be an awkward thing for a man and a woman, but it was not so with Emily and Case. They made love like they had been together for a very long time. When they had spent all their ardor, lost in each other's passion, they pulled away. Case rolled over on his back and put his arm around her. He was still breathing heavily when she let out a yelp so loud that it startled him. He jumped completely out of the bed.

"Danny Miller!" she shouted. "If you're still waiting for me, stop! I'm not coming back to you."

Case started laughing. "I think I understand what that means but why don't you explain it to me anyway?"

"My high school boyfriend told me he was going to wait for me until I came home from college. I told him he was wasting his time but he was not easily discouraged."

"Can't blame Danny for that. I'd wait four years for you too."

"You would?" she said, looking at him adoringly.

"I've been waiting for you all my life. I could do four years standing on one foot. I love you, Emily."

"You do?"

"Yeah, I do. And I'll prove it to you every day from here on out if you let me."

"I love you too," she said. "I suspected as much but I wanted to see if your love survived our first close encounter. I can't afford a broken heart."

"I won't break your heart, baby, I promise," he said, and he kissed her again."

"You want to go around again, cowboy?" she whispered in his ear.

"Yes, I do, but I'm not a cowboy. I raise alpacas."

"Then do me again, 'paca boy."

It was a month until Christmas. Case was planning a big Christmas at the ranch, but Emily had other obligations. "My folks are wanting me to come home for Christmas."

"But it's our first Christmas together, Em. I understand if you have to go home but Grandpa and Lupita were so excited to have you here with us this year."

"I was looking forward to it too, Case, but they're my parents, and I really want to see my brother."

"Can I come with you?" he said.

"Are you serious? You would do that?"

"If that would make you happy."

"It would make me very happy, darling. Oh, Case, thank you."

"I'll get the tickets. Where is the nearest airport to your home town?"

"Burlington International is the closest to Middlebury. Burlington is where the school is that I told you about."

"Then we can rent a car and drive to Middlebury."

"You always know the right thing to do or say to make my day."

"That's because I'm nuts about you," he said.

"I'm nuts about you too," she replied.

In the middle of December, Case picked up Emily at the dorm. He had a trailer hitched to his truck. In the trailer were two alpacas. Emily looked at them with surprise when she got into the truck.

"What are we doing?" she asked him.

"You remember the envelope I dropped in the gift basket at Mara's wedding?"

"Yes, I remember that."

"Well, that was an offer for two free alpacas, a male and a female. It was only good if they called and said they would take them. I got a call over the weekend from Jeremy telling me he would love to have them. Apparently, he's thinking about raising alpacas too. My guess is they will be pets for Mara. Anyway, we're going to deliver them."

"Any particular reason why you wanted me to go with you?" she asked.

"I can't stand to be away from you any more than I have to. Besides, it's a trip up to Evergreen and I didn't want to go alone."

"I'm glad you asked me to go along."

When they got to Jeremy and Mara's house, Mara led them to a fenced in area which Jeremy had built for their two new pets. There was also a shelter for them and an area filled with sand for the alpacas to roll in.

Mara hugged Emily and, when they were out of ear-shot of Case, she told her. "I'm so glad things are working out for you and Case. He's a changed a man, I guess he just needed the right woman to come along."

"Get this, Mara," Emily said. "He's going to Vermont with me for Christmas. I'm so thrilled about that."

"I never thought that would happen to Case Mac-Nicol but I'm glad I was wrong," Mara replied. "Congratulations to you both."

"Thank you, Mara, I'm happy for you too," Emily replied.

"Looks like Jeremy did his homework. The accommodations look very adequate. Please tell your husband that I am pleased and impressed with his effort," Case yelled to them as he was putting the animals in their pen.

"He wanted me to thank you for the gift," Mara said. "He's really excited about them." She invited them to stay for lunch but Case told her he had to get back.

"That was nice," Emily said, as they drove out of Evergreen.

Case just nodded.

"Looks like the fire may be under control."

"What do you mean?" he asked her.

"Mara's 'thing' for you. Before we got together, she told me that she was hopelessly in love with you. She never imagined that we'd end up together so she was very forthcoming about her feelings for you."

"Hmm," he said," If we ever slept together, I don't remember it now."

"Good, because she didn't have that hungry and needy look that she used to always have when you came around. So, I think she has the fire under control. I doubt that it will ever go out."

"Well, I hope it does. I hope that she and Jeremy are as happy as two people can be."

"I hope that too," she said.

They flew out of DIA at eight o'clock in the morning, on the twenty-third of December. The pilot came on the PA system and announced that they were crossing over Lake Champlain and would be on approach into Burlington Airport very shortly.

"Ah, Lake Champlain," Case commented. "Founded in 1609 by Samuel de Champlain, a French explorer. During the Revolutionary War, the lake was an important asset for allowing movement from the colonies to Canada and keeping New England a strong, connected force. It proved to be important in the military again in the War if 1812 for building ships, particularly out of Vergennes. The lake started to become a large tourist recreational entity around 1945 after the Second World War. It is now a vital part of the communities that surround it."

"Holy cow, Case," Emily exclaimed. "How in the world can you remember all that?"

"I didn't, I Googled it and saved it on my phone, I

had to glance at it a couple of times. I'd hoped to get through it all the way without looking at my notes, and impress you, but I couldn't remember it all.

"Well, I appreciate the effort. You might be interested to know that the lake is part of three counties, in New York, Vermont, and Quebec, and two countries USA and Canada."

"And I am glad to know that," he said.

They landed at Burlington International Airport, retrieved their baggage, and went to the car rental place. The car that Case had reserved was waiting for them.

"Holy shit, Emily, everybody here talks like you."

Emily laughed. "Did you think I was the only one?"

"Well, no, but I can understand you. They all talk a lot faster than you do. I had a hard time understanding what some of those folks were saying. One guy was ordering a 'hat dag' from a food cart."

"A hot dog," she said, being careful to enunciate clearly for him."

"Oh, that's what he was saying? Hey, here's our car, maybe you should drive," he said, you know your way around here."

She got behind the wheel and headed out to Highway Seven. "This will take us to Middlebury," she said.

"It's really pretty country, Emily."

"I think so, I loved growing up here. The people are mostly good natured and friendly."

"You came a long way from home just to save my life."

"That's so sweet, Case. If I had heard you say that before I got to know you, I would have thought it was bullshit."

"If I had said it before you got to know me it 'would' have been bullshit, honey."

She started laughing. "Are you enjoying the trip so far?"

"I am and I'm really looking forward to meeting your family and seeing the town you grew up in."

"Well, we're not too far away. Oh, I forgot to mention this but we won't be able to sleep together in my parents' house," she said.

"I figured that would be the rule. I'm okay with that."

"Good, thank you."

They entered the outskirts of Middlebury and she slowed down a bit.

"I'm glad you decided to drive so I can look at the town. The population of Middlebury is a just a little over eight-thousand people. And it's bigger than the state capitol," Case said.

"Google?"

"Yes, I wanted to learn about your hometown before we got here. Wait, slow down, what's that building on the left?"

"That's Swift House, it's a B and B," Emily told

him. "But that house is the registration office. The inn is just around the corner."

"I love that house, I'm going to build us one just like it in the east pasture on the ranch."

"Really?" she said incredulously.

"If you want one like that."

"What's wrong with your apartment?"

"I wouldn't want you to have to live in that. Oh! What's that, it looks like a church."

"That's the United Methodist Church. Watch now, on the right is the Town Hall Theater and right across the street is the Inn on the Green."

"This is the coolest town I've ever seen, Emily, it really is."

She was enjoying watching him get so excited about a place he'd never been before. He was like a child at a playground, trying to see everything at once.

"We're going to turn right on Cross Street and this bridge goes over Otter Creek."

"How far are we from your house?"

"Not far. The next street is Main and I'm going left here and veering left at this Y onto South Street. My house is just a few blocks away."

"Time to face the music," he said.

Emily had called home when they were just getting into the town. So, when she pulled into the driveway, they were standing on the porch with Emily's brother, Murphy.

Murphy ran to Emily first and Case went up on the porch to meet her folks.

"I assume you are Mister MacNicol," Norman said.

"No, sir, that's my grandfather's name, I'm Case MacNicol, call me Case," he said, reaching for Norman's hand, and they shook.

Norman nodded his head. "And this is Edna, Emily's mother."

He shook her hand as well. "I'm really glad to meet you both. I've heard a lot about you."

"Well, we've heard a lot about you too, Case," Norman said.

Emily came along with her brother. "Murph, this is my guy, Case.

"The boy looked at him with some suspicion but then held out his hand. "Hello, Mister Case," he said, "my name is Murphy Quarters. I'm glad to meet you."

"Well, I'm glad to meet you too, Murphy. Your sister has told me a lot about you."

After they went inside, the four of them sat down at the table. Edna Quarters had made a pot of coffee and she brought Case and Norman a cup and set the milk and sugar on the table.

"My daughter prefers tea so I will be right back after I heat up a cup for her."

Case put his index finger and thumb together, as if he were holding a cup of tea, and extended his pinky and jiggled it in front of Emily.

"What?" she said, smiling at him.

"You're having a spot of tea, like a fancy English lady?"

"Case keeps me laughing all the time, Mom. He pretends to be rough and unrefined but it's all an act. He actually does have manners."

"You told us that and now that I've met him, I can see it's true," Norman added.

Murphy came and sat in the chair next to Emily. He kept studying Case. "Are you Emmy's boyfriend?" he asked.

"Well, that's the job I applied for and she told me I got the job, so yes, Murphy, I am your sister's boyfriend."

Murphy continued talking and his mother was starting to get nervous of what he might say.

"Do you love Emmy?" Murphy asked him.

"Yes, Murphy, I do, I love her very much."

"And I love him right back, Murph," Emily said. "Now why don't you and I go up to your room and you can show me what you've been working on at school."

Norman and Edna wanted to know all about the ranch in Colorado. They talked for several hours and Case gave them a complete synopsis on the care and feeding of alpacas, of managing an alpaca business, and what it was like to grow up and live in Colorado.

As he talked, they could see the passion he had for his life and for his only family, his grandfather and Lupita. When he started talking about Emily, a similar passion came over him. He softened and lost the jocular, macho persona that he so obviously tried to project.

"She's the love of my life. I never had so much as a thought about loving a woman, or even being around one for more than a few hours at a time, before I met Emily."

"You know about her obligation to the school and hospital in Burlington, don't you?" Norman said.

"I do, and that's part of why I fell in love with her. I never had that kind of courage. I've always been dedicated to the ranch and to my grandfather, but to drive yourself the way Emily has done so you can help others, I just never knew people like that existed. She's just a very special person."

"What will you do when she comes back here to work? She has a four-year obligation, you know."

"I'll wait for her if that's what she wants me to do."

Emily came downstairs and joined them at the table. "You guys have been talking for hours. Case's jaws must be tired by now. He's not usually a big talker."

"We were pushing him pretty hard to tell us about his ranch and everything in Colorado," Edna said.

"Murph fell asleep but I don't think he'll be asleep very long. Case and I were talking about taking everyone out to dinner, if you don't have any other plans."

"I don't mind fixing dinner at home, Emily," Edna said.

"We'd really like to go out if you don't mind. I'd

like to see more of this town. Emily gave me a partial tour on the way in," Case said. "I Googled for the best restaurant in town and one came up that sounds interesting. It's called Fire and Ice. How does that sound?"

"It's pretty expensive Case, Norman said, we've been there once."

"How's the food?"

"The food is really good but it's very expensive."

"It's Christmas, and Emily and I brought gifts for everyone, Emily helped me pick them out because I don't know you guys, but we didn't have a lot of time. I'd like to take you all out as my Christmas gift."

"You might as well humor him, Dad. When he gets an idea like this, he won't give up until you do," Emily said."

"Thank you, baby," Case said. He noticed that Norman reacted strangely to his calling Emily, "baby." Maybe he was just over protective of his daughter or there was something about terms of endearment he didn't like. The Quarters were strange-acting people, he thought, very aloof and stand-offish, humorless. They rarely laughed at anything.

It was, perhaps because of their having to raise a child with autism or maybe the guilt they felt at wanting to abandon that responsibility in the beginning. He wouldn't waste much time trying to analyze them. He loved their daughter and that was all he needed to know about them.

They agreed to go to dinner, and it turned out to be a pleasant affair. The restaurant was plush, with extreme ambiance and great food.

Emily pulled him aside later and thanked him for being so nice to her parents. "It was wonderful of you to do this for them, for us. I appreciate it and I know they do too. My parents are New Englanders, we are typically just not as outgoing and gregarious as you westerners."

"What's that word mean?"

"Oh, it means outgoing and friendly."

"So, you used outgoing twice?" he said, smiling at her mischievously.

"You're pulling my leg, Case, you knew what that word meant."

"Well, they're such nice legs to pull, I just had to."

"You'll have to wait until we get back home to pull anything on me. I'm sorry."

"Back home? Did you just say back home?"

"I expect it will be someday," she said.

"Home for me is wherever you are, Emily."

"Now don't make me start crying."

"I'm sorry but it's the truth."

"I love you, Case."

"I love you too, Em."

Christmas day came and went. Case and Emily drove to Burlington, caught their flight back to Denver, and retrieved his truck from long-term parking. "Do you need to go by your dorm for anything?"

"No," she said. "Just get me to a bed."

"There's a bed in your dorm room isn't there?"

"A bed with you in it," she said.

"Oh, yes, ma'am. I know just where there is a bed that fits that description." They slept until the next morning and awoke to the sound of Lupita's knocking on the door informing them that she had breakfast ready in the house.

January came and the weight of their impending separation began to torment them both. Their lovemaking was more intense and more often it was almost as if each time they had together might be the last. Although their passion for each other did not wane, they seemed more desperate. Finally, he faced the inevitable.

"We have to talk about it, baby."

"I know, but it hurts so much for me just to think about it," she said. "What are we going to do?"

"We have two options, as I see it. One, you can give up your plans to leave Colorado and stay here and marry me and live happily ever after. I could pay them off for the money they spent on your schooling. But I don't think you would live happily ever after if you reneged on your obligation. I would not ask you to do that. I wouldn't 'let' you do that because I think it would ruin our marriage."

"You're right, I could not do that. It's a matter of honor. I made a promise. And it's not the money they care about, it's me, they want."

"I understand that. That leaves us with option two.

We get married and I wait for you. I'll fly up to Vermont every so often and spend a week with you. When you get a vacation, you can come home and spend it with me."

"Let me think on it, Case. We still have four months before we have to make a final decision. Something may happen in that time that could change things."

"I don't think anything is going to change," he said.

"I'd still like to wait before we get to that."

"Okay, honey, whatever you think."

January was the MacNicols' annual evening out to celebrate the birthday of their faithful housekeeper, Lupita Hernandez. Case reserved a table for four at the BBG. Martin was very accommodating, seating them at a table near the dance floor at Case's request.

Case, Emily, James and Lupita had their dinner and a few beers and Lupita was feeling her oats. Case went over, put five dollars in the juke box, and selected a variety of songs for them. When a slow song came on, he stood up.

"It's time for our dance," he said and held out his hand.

Emily started to stand up. "Not you, Em, this is my annual dance with Lupita. It's a family tradition."

The little woman followed him out to the dance floor and he twirled her the same way he had twirled Emily around the first time they had danced. He took her in his arms and they started waltzing across the dance floor.

Emily watched from the table. "What an amazing,

selfless man your grandson is, Mister MacNicol. Every time I'm with him, he does something that totally blows me away."

"Lupita raised him from the age of five. He loves her as the only mother and grandmother he's ever known. And stop calling me mister. My name is James or Grandpa."

"I'm sorry, I forgot," she said. "I'll start calling you Grandpa if that's okay."

"That's my preference, young lady."

"Then it's a done deal," she said.

The song was over and Case and Lupita were waiting for another one. A song by Bruno Mars called "Marry You" came on and the two of them started jitterbugging. Emily was beside herself with joy. She got up and took James's hand.

"Dance with me, Grandpa," she said.

He tried to resist but she would have none of it, pulling him out of his seat toward the dance floor.

Emily started twirling and shaking her butt to the up-beat music and James made a feeble attempt to copy her moves with no success.

"Aw, hell, I can't do this," he said. He put his arm around Emily, pulled her close, and started doing the Texas Two-Step across the floor. It was too slow a dance for the music but they did it. Applause went up all over the restaurant and bar.

Back at the table, James was worn out and Case was

laughing. "I bet that's the first time anyone has done the Texas Two-Step to a Bruno Mars song," he said.

"Or jitterbugged to a Bruno Mars song," Emily countered. "How did you learn how to jitterbug, Case?"

"Lupita taught me when I was a boy. We used to dance all the time to music on the radio."

Case took Emily to dance again and, as they moved together, she looked up at him and smiled. "This is the man I saw the first time we danced. In spite of everything the dorm girls had told me about you, I saw a different person. I saw the same man you are tonight. Watching you dance with Lupita made me really understand why I fell in love with you. Well, that and your work in the bedroom."

"You mean the way I remodeled my apartment?"

"No, the other kind of work. You know what I meant."

"You make love easy, baby," he said. "What will I do without you when you leave?"

"Just keep loving me," she said. "That's how I am going to cope with being away from you."

Emily had begun receiving emails from the Burlington Group, inquiring about her start-to-work date. They asked if she planned to take the summer off before starting to work full time. As much as she would have loved to spend the summer with Case, she nixed the idea. The sooner she began her job, the sooner her obligation would be satisfied and she could go home for good.

She started searching for an apartment online. She wanted to be close to the job but needed something cheap. A one-bedroom would be sufficient. No one would be staying with her, except Case when he came for a visit. She would try and fly back to Colorado every few months if she could afford it. She didn't want Case to pay for everything for her. She knew he would if she asked him, or even if she didn't, but she would remain adamant about that.

Case asked her to marry him, before she went back to Vermont, but Emily told him no.

"I want to wait until my commitment to the job is over," she told him. "Once I become your wife, my whole life will be dedicated to you, to you and me, and our children if we are so blessed but right now I can't make that promise. You deserve a full-time wife and I can't be that woman right now."

"I'm going to wait for you, Emily, no matter how long it takes or how hard it gets for me. I respect what you have to do and I want to marry you now but I'll accept what you decide," he said.

"I have to give this job everything I have and everything I am. I'm not suggesting that you won't be on my mind every day and every night, but I can't be torn between being a wife and keeping the commitment I made. I wish I were not so obligated but if I had not done what I did, I would never have met you. Then I would have no life at all, anyway."

"Okay, darling," he said. "You always make more sense than I do. You're thinking with you head and I'm thinking with my heart."

"And I love you for it. Let's get engaged if you want to, I would love that."

"Of course, I want to. Let's go downtown and I'll buy you a ring."

"Then I'll have something to show the world I belong to you."

"And I'll have a permanent smile on my face to show I belong to you."

They both laughed and he kissed her.

After graduation, Emily packed her things and put them in her car. She drove out to the ranch and moved into Case's apartment to spend her last week in Colorado, for a long while, with him.

The next morning, he saddled his horse, helped her up on the back behind him, and rode out to the hill where he and his grandpa used to go to talk when Case was a kid. He sat down with Emily on the same rock ledge and pointed south.

"It's too cloudy today but when it's really bright and clear, you can see Pikes Peak from here. My grandpa and I sat right here where we're sitting and he taught me everything I needed to know about life and family and good manners. He's a rough-cut man but he has more wisdom than any man I've ever known."

"I can see you in your grandfather, and I can see him

in you. Your grandpa is a picture of how you will be one day," she said.

"I want to grow old with you right here on this ranch. It's your home too, now."

"I won't be gone long."

"It will be an eternity," he said.

When they came down from the hill, he rode over to the east side of the property. "Here is where I'm going to build our house. I'm going to contact an architect in Vermont and get a set of construction plans for that house we saw when we first got into Middlebury."

"You were serious about that, weren't you?"

"I was dead serious, I love that house. Would you like that?"

"I think it would be wonderful, a little bit of Vermont in Colorado. Yes, I would love that too."

On the day she left, he printed out directions from the Google map for her to get back home. They loaded all her stuff in her car and Lupita made her a basket of sandwiches and pastries and such. James and Lupita said their goodbyes and went back into the house.

Case cautioned her about not trying to drive if she got sleepy, not to drive too fast and not to stop at night anywhere but in a rest stop.

"Okay, Daddy," she said, "I'm a big girl now. I'll be okay."

They kissed for the last time in what would be a long and lonely time for both of them."

Case watched as her Ford Focus drove out onto Magnolia Road and headed out of his life.

CHAPTER 9

The Colchester

Emily rented a studio apartment on Union Street. It was nine hundred dollars a month, which was a little steep, she believed, but it was clean and cozy and had free Wi-Fi so she'd be able to use her laptop to stay in touch with Case and her folks.

She found an auto service center, and had her car serviced, and went shopping for some new clothes to wear on the job. Her first meeting since she'd gotten back, had gone well. She would be working for both Mrs. Winters and for Doctor Shelby, dividing her time between the school and the hospital as each one's needs demanded. She would be a salaried employee with full benefits, holidays off, and a two-week vacation a year.

Her starting salary would be $65,000.00 a year.

Emily had not expected that she would make that much money. She basically had no idea what the job would pay and had not even speculated on it. Doctor Shelby assured her that she would receive increases on a yearly basis. She managed not to show her elation when told about the money. She just thanked him and assured him that she would do whatever they expected of her and more.

The first thing she did when she left the meeting was call Case. "You won't believe how much money I'm making, darling," she told him.

"If it's not more than minimum wage, then you get your lovely butt back in your car and come back home to me, you hear me?"

"Guess how much," she insisted and giggled like a teenager."

"Seventy-Grand," he said. "It better be seventy-grand."

"No, but your close. I'll be making sixty-five thousand dollars a year. But I'll get yearly raises."

"That's wonderful, Em, you're worth every nickel and I'm so proud of you."

"I miss you already, Case, and I've only been gone a week."

"I know, I miss you too but it's for a good cause. That's what I keep telling myself. I'm not going to repeat the old line I always hear people say in times like this."

"What line is that?" she asked.

"It'll be over before you know it, because I know it won't be."

"I get two weeks of vacation a year. The whole staff practically, takes off at Christmas so I'll spend that week with my parents but I'm going to take the other week in the summer and come home to see you, if that's okay."

"I'll have to check my schedule and see if I can clear up some time for you but, of course that's okay, silly. You don't even have to ask that," he said, laughing.

"I wish it were summer now," she said.

"I do too but summer will be here before you know it."

The facility was located on Colchester Avenue in Burlington and was referred to simply as The Colchester. Before Emily began actually working with autistic children, Mrs. Winters thought that, due to her previous work with her brother, it might be best if she began teaching other staff members how best to interact with the kids. She brought two young women into Emily's office on her second day.

"Emily, this is Sarah Peterson and Patty Thomas. They will be your staffers for now. Eventually we will be hiring more people in the near future but we don't want to overload you right out of the gate."

Emily shook hands with both of the girls. "Hi, Sarah, Hi, Patty, I'm happy to meet you both. Are you both from this area?"

"I'm from Burlington, Miss Quarters," Sarah Peterson said. "I graduated from high school last year. I couldn't go to college—grades were not good enough and my family can't afford to send me."

"Well, for goodness sake, call me Emily. And you can learn a lot on the job. I'm sure you'll work out fine."

"And I'm Patty Thomas," the other girl said. "Pretty much the same story with me, high school and no college."

"Don't let that slow you down. I'll teach you everything you need to know to do your job here."

Sarah was about the same height as Emily, had short blonde hair, and was heavier. The other girl, Patty was taller than they were and skinny. She had brown hair like Emily's and about the same length. Both were congenial young women and both seemed very happy to have the opportunity to be learning a job. Emily learned from them later that their families were not well off and needed the extra income the girls could provide. She began their training immediately.

"First, speak directly to the patient in simple terms. If you ask or tell them something and get a blank look, then re-word your comment, perhaps using simpler language or visuals. Don't try to give them too much to think about at one time. Be very specific and don't leave anything open to their own interpretation. Use as few words as possible to get your point across."

There were eight patients in the class and Emily soon

got to know them intimately. To her, they were all like Murphy. She felt passion and love for each one but kept her interaction with them on a professional level. She was firm but not overbearing. The parents played an important part in the lives of an autistic child, and Emily worked as hard and almost as often with the parents as with the child.

"Don't give long and complicated instructions, keep tasks short and simple but very specific. Tell them: open books, get pens. When you want them to stop, say: close books, put your pens down. You will have to teach them basic social skills like keeping out of another person's personal space. Many of them have no concept of how close to stand to another person with whom they are conversing. Be gentle yet firm. Teach them to back off to a respectful distance. They will eventually understand. We'll take them outside, weather permitting, as a group when at least two of us are available to go along. You two will discover that this is demanding work but it is rewarding. Most of them like to go outside. Some do not and we will encourage them to go but will not force them."

"Should we ask them what they want to do on occasion or always have a plan for the day?" Sarah asked her.

"You can ask them but have a choice for them to make. For instance, ask them 'do you want to read or draw?' Don't ask, 'what do you want to do now?' That can confuse them sometimes. They need structure so a

daily routine is very important. Even their free time has
to be structured. Repeat your instructions to be certain the
child understands it. And above all, be patient. Remember always that, if a child gets frustrated or angry, it's
most likely directed at something or someone other than
you. Call the child by his or her name to build their respect for you. Just never respond out of frustration or
with sarcasm. If they do something wrong and you respond 'Great' sarcastically, they will not understand and
think you really mean 'Great'. And remember that, with
autistic children, any change in routine can trigger an
anxiety attack."

Emily paused for a quick breath. "We cannot avoid
this ever happening but with diligence and proper behavior on our part we can minimize it. Just keep in your
minds that the children did not choose this life for themselves, it's not their fault they are the way they are."

It was demanding work and not everyone had the
temperament for it. Emily continued with Sarah and Patty, until Patty was transferred to the hospital facility to
fill a gap there. The facility gave Emily what help they
could from time to time.

In the time that she worked with Sarah the two of
them became good friends and Emily gained Sarah's respect. It was on a field trip to a local park that Sarah
learned why the Burlington people had been so enamored
with Emily Quarters. A boy named Michael, who suffered with multiple personality disorder, began talking to

himself while under Sarah's supervision. He was insisting that one of his alter egos, an individual he called Tommy was calling him bad names and wouldn't stop.

"Stop, stop Tommy," he continued yelling and nothing Sarah could do would calm him down. He was starting to make a scene and drawing attention to them. People around them were starting to become concerned.

"Do you want us to call nine-one-one?" a couple of them asked her.

"No," she replied, "I called my boss. She's close by with some other kids. She's on her way."

Emily arrived with the other kids in tow and assessed the situation. "What is it, Michael?" she asked him and he told her the same thing he had told Sarah.

"Make Tommy stop calling me names, Miss Quarters." The boy was crying now.

Emily suddenly shouted loudly, "Tommy, you stop calling Michael names right now! Do you understand me?"

The boy stopped crying and a smile came over his face. "Thank you, Miss Quarters."

Sarah just marveled that she had not known, or that it had not even occurred to her to do that.

A short time later, Doctor Shelby asked Emily to look at a case that had been sent to them from the CPS (Child Protective Services). A young boy named Calvin, who was given to fits of rage, had been expelled from school in the first grade and again in the second grade. He had failed both grades but had been passed on in the first and held back in the second, therefore, he was eight years old now and still in second grade. He was constantly in trouble with the school authorities.

"I would appreciate anything you can do to help me out with this boy, Emily. He may be a lost cause but I'm giving him to you as a last resort. CPS had removed the boy from his home. But after the parents petitioned to get him back, they relented, and now he is back at home. He keeps getting suspended from school. I'm afraid if we can't help him, he won't have much of a future."

"I'll do my best, Doctor," she told him.

"That's all I ask," Shelby replied.

She saw the boy first and asked his parents to stay in the waiting room until she called them. Calvin was a small boy, smaller than average, but he carried himself aggressively. There was a permanent grimace on his face. And he didn't seem capable of sitting still for very long at a time. She moved the chair from in front of her desk and slid it around to the side where the boy could sit close enough to her for more intimate conversation than was afforded from across and behind her desk. "Come and sit down by me, Calvin. Let's talk a while," she said.

The boy did as she told him but he remained uncomfortable at best.

"What do you like to do for fun?" she asked him. He shrugged his shoulders but did not speak. "What games do you like to play?" she continued.

"I like Minecraft sometimes and Angry Birds mostly."

"I like Angry Birds too," Emily said, "but I'm not very good at it. I never can hit any of the pigs."

The boy started to show some interest. "How do you know about Angry Birds?" he asked her, displaying a bit of skepticism.

"I used to play with my brother when I was younger but he always beat me."

"What color birds are your favorites?" he asked.

"I only learned how to use the red ones and the blue ones. I could lob the red ones right on top of the pigs pretty good, most of the time, but they were always hiding behind stuff, you know, walls and glass windows and—"

"You have to break that stuff up," he said.

"Yeah, I know but I was never very good at it. Can you show me?" She turned her computer around, Googled the game, downloaded it, and let Calvin set it up and start a game. "The blue bird turns into three little birds and break the glass windows," he told her.

"How do you make them turn into three birds?"

"Tap the screen like this." He showed her how to do it.

She and her brother Murphy had played the game for hours on end when she was taking care of him and teaching him. The truth was that Emily was still quite proficient at the child's game, though it had been many years since she had played it. However, for her purpose here, she thought it better therapy to play the student and let Calvin take the lead. It quickly became obvious that he was enjoying teaching his teacher how to play his game.

"The yellow bird is fast and can break a wood door. The black bird blows up if you tap the screen or, if you don't tap the screen and just let it hit something, it'll blow up after a little bit. The white bird drops an egg that blows up and knocks down a rock wall."

"My gosh, Calvin," Emily said, "how do you re-member all those different birds?"

"It's easy, Miss Quarters, and there's more." He went on to tell her about all the other colored birds and all the tasks they could perform.

Finally, Emily said she was ready. "Okay, Calvin, let's play."

They sat there playing the game for an hour. As she had done with her brother, Emily played just good enough to lose. With each win, Calvin became more ex-cited. His face was bright and the ever-widening grin on his face was a total surprise to Doctor Shelby, who looked in once to see how things were going. He gave Emily a thumbs up and quietly closed the door.

Before too long, Emily perceived that Calvin was slacking off and trying to let her win a game. It was a sweet thing, and she let him know. "Now, Calvin, I know you are trying to let me win one game, and it's very sweet of you but you are just better at this than I am. So don't worry about my feelings. I've had so much fun playing the game with you, even if I didn't win. I haven't had this much fun in a long time."

"I had fun too, Miss Quarters. Thank you for being so nice to me."

"You're going to be coming back to see me every week for a while so we'll get to be good friends. I look forward to seeing you again soon. And I'll be talking to your mom and dad too." The pleasant look on the boy's face went away at the mention of his parents and his demeanor changed as they came for him and walked out of the building with him.

"So, do you have any thoughts on Calvin Bishop? He seemed to be in great spirits when I looked in on you," Doctor Shelby asked Emily in a follow-up meeting.

"I think his problem is most likely parental related," she said.

Shelby just nodded. "Keep me informed, if you will."

"Of course, Doctor," she said.

The next time the Bishop family came in for their regular weekly appointment, Emily asked Sarah to keep Calvin occupied while she talked to his parents. The Bishops were not well off but neither were they a poor family.

Joe Bishop owned a welding shop and, according to what information Emily could gather from the people at The Colchester, he made a decent living, although his drinking diminished their enjoyment of his gainful pursuit of the American dream.

The story was typical, but Emily disliked sounding typical. Telling a parent that their child is an intelligent kid, but is not applying himself and is not living up to his full potential, sounds so trite and patronizing. But in Calvin's case it was the truth. She told them about the game she had played with him and how adept he was at playing the game.

"It's a kid's game, "Joe Bishop said, "don't mean nothin'."

"But his ability to remember the most intricate details of the game, each color of every bird, and their individual abilities and tasks indicates a much higher level of intelligence than you may be aware of. He's a remarkable boy. I'd like to see you encourage that."

"And how do we do that?" Joe asked.

"Forgive me if I seem insensitive, but a child needs the interaction of both parents in his development. It would be helpful if both of you, especially you, Mister Bishop, took an interest in his schoolwork, helped him with his homework, and went to the parent-teacher meetings together. Let him know that you are heavily invested in his education, in his life, and in his future."

"The boy is either a dumbass or just plain lazy," Joe Bishop said.

Ida Bishop tried to correct him. "Now Joe, he's not a dumb boy."

"You shut up, Ida. The boy don't want to learn nothin'. Every time I try and help him he gets all mad and starts goin' off on me."

"And how do you handle discipline in those incidents, Mister Bishop?" Emily asked.

"I take my belt to him. I'm not gonna take that kind of guff from a kid."

"Do you think that's the best way to handle that situation, sir?"

"It's the best way for me."

"But do you think it's the best way to help Calvin?"

"Well, miss, the bible says, 'spare the rod and spoil the child,'" Joe said piously.

"I know, Mister Bishop.," Emily responded. "The bible also says 'Fathers, provoke not you children to wrath, but bring them up in the nurture and admonition of the Lord.' Ephesians Six: Four."

"I don't know what that means, miss, can you explain it to me?"

"There is a time for spanking a child, Mister Bishop, but it should not replace good parenting. Proverbs Fifteen-One says, 'A soft answer turns away anger.' Spanking should be a last resort, not the first reflexive response. Calvin is your son, your own flesh and blood. If you can take in the enormity and the wonder of that, I think you'll understand what a special relationship you have with Calvin. You're an adult. Calvin looks to you to help him deal with the unknowns of life. You have to ask yourself,

Do you want your son coming to you when he has a need for help or information or something else he doesn't know how to handle, or do you want him relying on strangers?"

"But I'm just not very good at that sort of thing, Miss Quarters. It just don't come natural to me."

"It doesn't come natural to a lot of people, Joe, but it's worth pursuing if it will help your son. I'm telling you, Calvin is a good boy, and he's smart, really smart. You are the key to getting him through the trouble he's having."

"I wasn't expecting you to jump back at me with the bible. You seem to know a lot more about it than I do. How did you—"

"My mother taught me when I was a girl. I have to be honest and say I haven't kept up with it, but some of the passages I learned a long time ago have stayed with me."

"Well, it sure shut me up, and I can already see how you've helped my boy. Can you teach me how to handle him so we can get along better? I want to be a good dad. I'm just being the way my old man was with me. If that's wrong, then I want to change if you think I can, Miss Quarters."

"I know you can, Joe, and call me Emily. We'll have the regular weekly session with you, Ida, and Calvin. It'll be a family thing. I think we can all benefit from this," Emily said.

"Thank you, Emily," Joe said." I appreciate what you're doin' for us.""

The congeniality between coworkers at the facility often served to ease the tension caused by the seriousness of the job. The ladies who worked in the office were very close friends and spent a lot of time together off the job.

Marie was the receptionist and the prettiest of the office staff. She had short blonde hair, was about Emily's height and build, but at least ten years older. She was married and yet she flirted as if she wasn't. Gayle was the bookkeeper, an older Black lady who was witty and always laughing at one thing or another.

Lunchtime was always like a "hen house," as the male employees liked to refer to the break room activities. The women talked about their husbands and boyfriends, or lack thereof, and pondered over the ones they didn't marry or go out with. Marie, at thirty-five, was still an attractive woman and clearly in a strained marriage. She was often propositioned by salesmen who came into the office and by men in the local bars, where some of the staffers went on Fridays after work for a few drinks. To date, she had not gone over the line and engaged in an extra marital affair. At least she had not, as far as anyone at the office knew or suspected.

Judy was the company typist, a short unimpressive girl of twenty-one with dark brown hair, who only occasionally joined in the conversation. April was a pretty woman, thirty-two years old with short red hair that she was proud of. She was taller than Emily but heavier. And then there was Agnes, a sixty-two-year-old gray-haired woman who handled all the billing. Agnes rarely stopped talking and often complained about how the managers mismanaged the facility.

Sarah had seen the picture of Case that Emily had on her phone and made the mistake of mentioning it one day at lunch. Then everyone wanted to see "Emily's man." Reluctantly, Emily pulled up the picture and passed it around.

Gayle virtually whooped. "Oh my God, girl, you mean to tell me you left this man in Colorado alone and came here without him. Are you crazy?"

"I trust him," Emily said. "And he trusts me."

"You can't trust any man, Emily," Gayle retorted. "If a man has a pecker, he can't be trusted."

"Well, if a man doesn't have pecker, he's a woman, and you can't trust a woman either," Agnes added and they all laughed.

"So, when are you getting married?" April asked her.

"When my obligation to The Colchester is fulfilled," Emily said.

"Wow, you still have quite a bit of time left on that, don't you?"

"About two and a half years. It seems like it will never end."

"Tell them how you guys met," Sarah said to Emily.

"They don't want to hear that," Emily said.

"Yes, we do," they all shouted at the same time.

Emily sighed and nodded her head. "Okay, well it was kind of strange. We had seen each other a couple of times before but it actually happened at the wedding of a friend of mine who lived in the same dorm I was in. Case asked me to dance, and then after that he took me to his ranch. I found out later that he had never taken a girl to his ranch before. He told me later that he had fallen in love with me after seeing a picture of me that was taken at a concert at the nightspot where we hung out. I know that sounds crazy but that's what he said. I didn't trust him at first because he had quite a reputation with the women, and I thought he was just trying to get me into bed. But he has these most amazing green eyes. Once you look into those eyes, you are mesmerized, and you have no control over yourself anymore."

"Oh, hell, woman. I got to meet this magic man," Gayle said. "When is he coming to see you again?"

"Probably around Christmas but I might go to see him. We haven't decided yet."

"I just have one question for you, Emily," Agnes said. "How is he in the sack?"

Emily smiled mischievously. "Now, Agnes, I'm not the kind of girl who kisses and tells."

"Oh, come on, humor an old woman's fantasy, Emily," Agnes replied, and they all started laughing.

"I'll tell you this much, Agnes. Case knows how to hit the right spot."

They all giggled like a bunch of schoolgirls, even Agnes.

When Emily got back to her apartment that afternoon she had an e-mail from Case.

~ Hi, baby, still missing you. Rudy says hey. I sent off for the construction plans for that house we saw in Middlebury. I want to have it ready for you when you get back but I want you to have a say in picking out all the paint colors, outside, trim, and inside, walls cabinets kitchen, etc. everything.

Maybe you can come back home for Christmas and we can make some decisions. I've already picked out a spot for the house and built a new gate and road to the location. But I have to have your input before I can do too much.

I've only been to the BBG twice in the last six months to have lunch with Martin. He thinks I have abandoned him but I told him I would stop in more often. Without you here, it just isn't much fun. I have to get back to work now. I love you, Case

The reality of her situation struck her with every email she received from Case, although she was happy to get them. And as the loneliness engulfed her, she thought about how much worse it would be without the modern technology of instant communication. If she had to wait for a letter to arrive in the mail, she was certain she would lose her mind. As she lay in bed, she chuckled about Case's sense of humor. Telling her that his prized red alpaca had said hello to her was just like him. She ached from the loneliness and quietly prayed that somehow it would go away.

She could not even think of reneging on her obligation, but she was not yet even half way through it and her empty arms reached out for him in the darkness every night.

The weekly sessions with the Bishops were like the answer to prayers. Joe Bishop became a changed man and had begun to treat his son and his wife like the father and husband they'd always needed. He thanked Emily profusely every time they came for counseling. Once time, he even started crying in front of them all when he started telling about his having a religious epiphany. His wife and son hugged him and told Emily how grateful they were to her for helping them.

In their final session, when Joe tried to express to Emily how much she had done for them, he broke down again.

"You did it, Joe, you. I was just here to sort of point the way. I didn't do it for you, I couldn't do it for you. You and Ida and Calvin all worked together to save your family. It's a wonderful thing you've done. I'm happy for you."

Doctor Shelby asked Emily to come to his office for a follow-up meeting on the Bishop situation. Jason Shelby was sixteen years older than Emily and had lost his wife to cancer five years earlier.

He was a desperately lonely man, as lonely as Emily was but, unlike her, he was lonely with no cure for his loneliness. His attraction to her had slowly turned into a secret burning love.

But it was a love that he would never express because he knew her story, and he'd seen the look in her eyes when she talked about the man from Colorado. So, he buried any thoughts he might have of pursuing a relationship with her.

"Have a seat, Emily," he said, as she walked into his office.

"Thank you, Doctor," Emily said. "What's up?"

"I just wanted to tell you that you are an amazing young woman, so wise beyond your years that you defy logic."

"Well, that's the way I like to start the day. Thank you, Doctor Shelby. To what do I owe this compliment?"

"The Bishops," he said. "For all intents and purposes, to coin a cliché, you absolutely worked a miracle with that family. I'm proud of you and The Colchester is proud of you."

"It really did work out well for them. I'm happy about that."

"I'd like to take you and Miss Peterson to lunch today as a small, very small, token of our appreciation for all the good work you've done for us. We can get couple of the nurses to fill in for you while we're off the premises."

"I think that would be nice, Doctor, Thank you. I'll go tell Sarah as soon as we are finished here."

They went to an upscale restaurant near the waterfront, and Doctor Shelby reiterated to Emily how proud he was of both her and Sarah, for their service to the community, in the time they had been at The Colchester. Sarah noticed that as he spoke to them, most of the doctor's attention was directed at Emily.

"Doctor Shelby has a 'thing' for you, Emily," she said after they were back at work.

"Oh, come on, Sarah, you don't really believe that, do you?"

"I know it. He couldn't take his eyes off you, all during lunch. And the look in his eyes said more than just appreciation for the work you do here. I was just there because he is too much of a gentleman to ask you out by yourself. He knows you're engaged."

"Hmm, I didn't see it. Maybe I just wasn't paying attention but I thought he was being very professional. He's never said or done anything that made me think that he felt that way."

"He wouldn't then, would he? You work together. It would be inappropriate. But he lost his wife a few years ago, and anyone can see he's a lonely man. You're the perfect woman for a man like Doctor Shelby."

"I am," Emily said, surprised, "the perfect woman?

What, pray tell, makes me the perfect woman for Doctor Shelby?"

"Think about it," Sarah said. "You're engaged to the love of your life, everyone knows that, and yet you leave him for a four-year commitment, to a job, that you made before you met him. You never go out or even glance sideways at other men. You're beautiful and intelligent." Emily nodded in agreement, smiling. "I mean if Doctor Shelby didn't fall in love with you, I'd have to think he was gay."

"You may be right, Sarah. I just hope he doesn't act on it because that could get awkward. I'd hate to hurt him," Emily said. "But thanks for telling me that. I really had not noticed it."

"Well, we deserved the lunch anyway. We are an outstanding team of professionals," Sarah said.

"Indeed, we are," Emily replied.

Then they high-fived each other and went back to work.

CHAPTER 10

High Mountain Meadow

C ase picked out a location for the new house he intended to build for him and Emily, and all the little Cases and Emilies that might come along in the future, to live in. He built a new gate and a gravel road, which would be used for the construction work and would eventually be replaced with an asphalt, or maybe a brick road, sometime later. The sign over the gate read *Emily's Meadow*. He knew it sounded presumptuous but he didn't care. He thought Emily would like it. He wasn't going to tell her about the sign until she came and saw it the first time herself.

While driving down to Denver to deliver wool to the spinner, he was listening to an oldies station on the radio.

A song came on, by a group called Front Range, called
"High Mountain Meadow." Case took an instant liking to
the song because it seemed to speak to everything he
loved about Colorado. He couldn't remember the words
so after he got back home he Googled the song and found
the lyrics. He immediately copied the lyrics and emailed
them to Emily.

*~ Hello beautiful, still missing you. I hope you are
okay. First off, I love you. Second: I heard a song on the
oldies station today that made me think of you. It's a song
about Colorado and a guy who is going to build a home
for the woman he loves. Sound familiar? I've pasted the
lyrics below. Here are the lyrics to the song. I hope you
like it as much as I do.*

HIGH MOUNTAIN MEADOW

*When the springtime comes dancing through the Rockies
And the oak and the aspen turn to green,
We can hitch up the horses to the wagon
And I'll take you to the mountains,
to a place you've never seen.*

*Through the long and lonely winter we have courted,
Sharing dreams and walking through the snow.
We will marry when the rivers start a' running,
And in a high mountain meadow, I'll build you a home.*

And our songs will echo through the mountains
As we spend our time together, all alone.
When the springtime comes dancing through the Rockies,
In a high mountain meadow, I'll build you a home.

Now the coals in the fire are brightly glowing
Like the love that lies warm within our hearts.
In your eyes, I can see the fire a glowing
As we talk about the springtime,
when we never more will part.

And our songs will echo through the mountains,
As we spend our time together, all alone.
When the springtime comes dancing through the Rockies,
In a high mountain meadow, I'll build you a home.

That's it, Darling, that's our song. I'll be singing it
until you come back to me, then we'll sing it together. I
love you,
Case

When Case turned twenty-five he became eligible to receive his father's inheritance. Case's grandpa had been instrumental in his son's adding the stipulation that Case would not receive the money until he had reached that age. His reasoning for that was that he, James MacNicol, had known that his own son, Case's father Casey, had not been responsible enough before that age to handle large sums of money. And as it turned out, James was glad his son had followed his advice.

James would not have wanted his grandson to come into a large sum of money at an earlier age than twenty-five because he believed the boy would have squandered it before he reached the age of eligibility his father had set for him.

But now Case was twenty-five years old but, more importantly, he had met the woman he intended to marry and spend the rest of his life with. The boy was already rich but didn't know it. James MacNicol had paid him a decent salary for his work on the ranch but had placed his share of the profits in an annuity that had grown substantially over the years since he'd become a partner in the enterprise.

His investment, plus his ownership share in the ranch, was well over 500,000 dollars, not counting the land the ranch was on, and the inheritance from his father came to a million-four. Case took it in stride when his grandfather presented him with the numbers.

The money itself meant little to him. It was what it could do for him and Emily that really mattered to him.

"I want you to think about something, Case." his grandfather said to him.

"Okay, Grandpa, what's that?"

"I know you miss your girl, and I know you have been having a hard time being away from her. If you want to, you can go and stay there with her for as long as you need to. You can stay until she's ready to come back here if you want to."

"I can't leave you alone to run the ranch by yourself, Grandpa."

"Horseshit, boy, I can hire a foreman to fill in for you until you get back. It's a sacrifice we can make, if necessary."

"But I've never been away from you and Lupita for a single day my whole life, except when I went to Vermont with Emily. I don't know if I can do that. What if you get sick or something?"

"They got airplanes that fly from Vermont to Denver, don't they?" James said.

"Yeah, but this ranch has been my life all my life."

"That girl is your life now, son. You need to be with her."

"Let me think on it, Grandpa. I want to start the construction on the house. And I want to bring her up here around Christmas to help choose paint colors and other things that men usually let women decide on. I don't want to tell her right now that I might do that. I've never lived in another state. I don't know if I can live on any air but mountain air."

"Now you're bullshittin' me," James said. "I wouldn't tell her anyway. If you decide to do it, then just do it and surprise her. Think how that would make her feel if you just showed up with all your stuff in your truck and told her you were moving there to be with her."

Case appeared to be thinking for a few moments. "By golly, you're right, Grandpa. If I do decide to do it, that's what I'll do. I'll just show up and knock her socks off."

"And probably a lot of other articles of clothing as well," James said.

Case chuckled. "I bet you were something with the women when you were my age, Grandpa."

"I had my moments, son, I had my moments."

The concrete crew poured the slab for the house and covered it with Visqueen plastic waterproofing material and then with straw to enable the concrete to set in the cold weather. The framing would be up and the roof would be on and dried-in by the time Emily came for the Christmas holiday. Case had a long list of things for her to decide when she arrived.

The work continued on the ranch, and Case did not shirk his duties because of the house. It was shearing time again, and he made his regular trips into Denver to deliver the wool to the spinners. He had some hats and sweaters and other pieces of wool clothing and accessories made from alpaca wool that he would ship to Emily's family in time for their Christmas.

Case made one of his rare trips into Boulder to see Martin at the BBG. They had lunch together in the restaurant, so Martin could be on hand if he were needed, and talked about what they called the "old days" before Emily.

"I remember those days of long ago," Martin said, poking fun at Case, "when you used to be a man, I mean."

"Yeah, me too," Case replied, "I told myself I was having fun."

"You were, weren't you?"

"Well, yeah, I was," Case said, and they both laughed loudly.

"Andrea's Angels have all moved on," Martin said. "There's a whole new flock of them in here every night now."

"Any of them ask for me?" Case said.

"No, I haven't heard any of them mention your name. I have to admit I was a little surprised."

"So, it looks like I was a legend in my own mind."

"Apparently so, but I'm happy for you, buddy." Martin received a phone call. "Hey, I have to take this, I'll be right back."

Case nodded.

"Hi, Case," a voice behind him said, "haven't seen you in a while. What's going on?" It was Angie, coming over to the table.

"I've been pretty busy, Angie. How have you been?"

"You never called me about that next time you promised me."

"I know, and I'm sorry about that. Some things just happened and got in the way. I really meant it at the time I hope you believe that."

"I heard you got married, Case, is that true?"

"I'm engaged, Angie. We're going to get married when Emily finishes her job in Vermont."

"So, she's not here with you?"

"No, but she's coming for Christmas. I'm building us a house at the ranch."

"I could keep you company in the meantime."

"I know you could, and it would be very good company Angie, but I can't. I'm sorry, I just can't. Had I not met Emily, I have to believe it would have been different for us. I really like you and I'm sorry about breaking it off like I did. It was inconsiderate on my part, but I fell pretty hard when I finally fell.

"It's okay, Case, as much as I was hoping to get in bed with you, I was sort of hoping you'd say that. It makes me realize what kind of man I want to marry, if one ever comes along like you for me."

"Well I hope he does, Angie, because he'll be a very lucky man. You're a beautiful woman, and a good woman, and whoever he may be, I hope he treats you like you deserve to be treated."

She looked like she was about to cry. "Thank you," was all she said and she walked away.

Martin returned to the table. "So where were we, Case?" he asked.

"Emily's coming for Christmas."

"I bet you're excited about that, huh?

"I am, I really miss her. I knew this deal she had was

going to be hard but I didn't realize it was going to be pure torture. I've never been in love before, I mean I've never been with a woman that I couldn't stand to be away from."

"I know how you feel," Martin said.

"It must be hell for you, buddy, I can't imagine what you must be going through."

"We're talking. I think that eventually she will come around. I have a vacation coming up and I'm thinking of going back to Indiana and having a serious talk with her about coming out here."

"I hope it works out for you," Case said.

"It has to, Case. If it doesn't pretty soon, then we only have one option. A marriage cannot survive like this forever."

"I hear you. I'm hoping for the best for you," Case said. "Emily and I are going to need some friends. I'd love for them to be you and Victoria."

"Thanks, buddy, I appreciate that."

Emily made a point never to check her personal email at work. She didn't want to be distracted by anything that Case might send her, preferring to open it up at night in the privacy of her apartment where she could contemplate, laugh or cry, or express whatever emotion seemed right for the occasion.

The song lyrics he sent made her long to be back at Magnolia Road Ranch with him. She wished she could hear the song. The words were so beautiful and she was not surprised that Case was drawn to the song. She wrote him a brief reply.

~ Yes, darling, it IS our song. Thanks a lot, now you've got me grieving for Colorado and the ranch. I'm so happy about the house. I wish I could be there to watch it go up. I am definitely planning to come home for Christmas. I will let you know my flight time so you can pick me up.

I got an attagirl from the head doctor, perhaps I should have said the administrator, for my work with the family of a boy with behavioral problems, no promotion or commendation in my file but just a 'Thanks' for a job well done, so to speak. Tell Grandpa and Lupita I said hello.

I love you
Your Emily

She got a ride from Sarah to the Burlington Airport, checked her bags, and passed through the security check and then had to wait an hour for her flight. Some passengers were pointing out the window and Emily turned to see an American Airlines plane taxiing up to the concourse. "Won't be long now," a man was telling his wife.

It seemed to take forever for them to start loading, but eventually she was in the boarding ramp. She found her seat and, as she had requested, it was an aisle seat. An elderly woman was seated next to her and the woman's husband was in the window seat. Emily hoped the woman would not be a talker because she was not looking forward to engaging in superficial and inane conversation for the next three hours and forty-nine minutes.

After the obligatory safety presentations and taxi to the takeoff position, the aircraft started rolling down the runway, lifted off, and roared over Lake Champlain. After a few minutes, it leveled off and seemed to turn a bit and, in Emily's mind, headed toward Colorado. She adjusted her seatback into the reclined position and leaned back, in hopes of taking a nap and waking up on descent into DIA. But the elderly woman in the next chair ruined that plan for her when she started talking to her.

"Why are you going to Denver, miss?" the woman asked.

It was not in Emily's nature to be rude to anyone, especially an older person, so she raised her seatback to the up position. "I'm going to spend Christmas with my fiancé and his family," she said.

"Oh, that's wonderful," the woman responded. "Are you from Colorado originally?"

"No, ma'am, I'm from Vermont, Middlebury. But I work in Burlington."

"And is your fiancé from Vermont too?"

"No, he's a rancher, Colorado native," Emily said.

"Oh, a cowboy."

Emily smiled. "He'd laugh if he heard you say that, but no, he's not a cowboy. He owns an alpaca ranch with his grandfather west of boulder. He's building a house for us on the property for when I come back to live there permanently."

The woman looked confused as if she didn't know what to say.

"Oh, I know it sounds strange but we met when I was going to the University of Colorado. I had made a commitment to the company I work for. You see, they helped me go to school to get my degree, and I agreed to work for them for four years, after I graduated, as a reimbursement. They pay me well and I'm almost halfway through my obligation. I'm going home now for Christmas and to help Case, that's my fiancé, pick out paint colors and cabinets, and stuff for the house. We are going to get married when I move back for good."

"And you trusted this man to wait four years and be faithful to you all that time?"

"Yes, yes, I do. He's an amazing man. Here's a picture of him." She pulled up a picture of Case on her phone.

The woman looked and her eyes twinkled. "Oh my," she said. "He certainly is a handsome young man. How did you two meet?"

"We met at a wedding of a friend of mine from my dormitory. It was kind of a 'love at first sight' sort of thing. But it's lasted for three years now."

"Well, you are both very lucky to have found each other. My husband and I are going to our son's house in

Colorado Springs to help him load up his things and come back home to Vermont."

Emily felt the dread of what the woman was going to say next. The woman's tone, and the husband's sullen demeanor, told her that it was not a happy time for them but Emily didn't want to ask. "So, your family is from Vermont?"

"Yes, we live in Burlington and our son grew up in Burlington. He met a girl from Colorado on a skiing trip and they fell in love and, well, it's been ten years now. They have three kids and their marriage fell apart. Linda, that's Joey's wife, met another man and wanted a divorce. Joey was devastated but he had to accept it. She gave up the kids to go with the other man. Joey is at least happy that he gets to keep his children but they have lived their lives in Colorado and don't want to leave. All Joey wants to do is get as far away from the bad memories as he can. He's a good father, and he will help the kids adjust."

"I'm so sorry to hear about your son's misfortune, Mrs…"

"Pearson, Emily Pearson, and my husband is Fred Pearson."

"My name is Emily too, Mrs. Pearson."

"Well, now that is a coincidence. I'm glad to have met you, Emily. I'll leave you alone now so you can finish your nap."

Emily woke up as the plane was on approach into

Denver International Airport. After de-boarding, she bid farewell to Mrs. Pearson and wished her good luck and then went to baggage claims to retrieve her belongings.

Standing outside baggage Claims, Case was waiting for her. He smiled when she saw him. She walked over to him and he hugged her. "I'm going to kiss you when we get in the truck but for now I just want to hold you," he said. "It seems like it's been years since I've held you."

"Oh God, how I've missed you, Case. I wish I could stay with you and never go back."

A few minutes of passion in his truck could not assuage their need for each other and, after she had caught her breath, Emily sighed. "You better get me to a bed Mister MacNicol, ASAP."

"You didn't nap on the plane?" he said, smiling at her.

"You know what I mean."

"You have to see the house first," he insisted.

"I love Boulder," she said as they approached the edge of the town. "And the Flatirons are so beautiful. I never thought I could love any place as much as I love Vermont but I do love it here. I think it's because you love it so much."

"I'd love any place you are, baby, even Texas, I suppose. Well, maybe not Texas. I don't know, if you were there—maybe."

They turned onto Magnolia Road and drew close to the ranch. "Now get ready, we're coming up on our gate.

I had a new gate built to get to our house." He stopped when he got to the entry, and she looked up and saw the sign.

"Emily's Meadow? Are you serious, Case? You named it after me? I don't know what to say. I'm over-whelmed. Will you never stop surprising me? I don't de-serve this. What did I do to deserve this, to deserve you?"

"Are you kidding me, baby? This is the least I can do for you after all you've done for me. You made me real-ize what a man is supposed to be. I was just a pile of dog shit in the cantaloupe patch until I met you. You gave me a reason to be happy." He drove on to the house with Bo-gie and Bacall escorting them.

"Dog shit in the cantaloupe patch?" she asked.

"It's a line from an old movie," he said.

"Really, what movie?"

"*Urban Cowboy*, John Travolta's Uncle Bob."

Emily nodded. "Oh, well, this is a wonderful honor and the house is beautiful. I want to go inside."

"Well, come on. It's sheet-rocked but not painted or anything but I'll show you the rooms. There are four bed-rooms upstairs and an extra one downstairs. The master bedroom, our bedroom, has a patio on the back so we can sit outside and look at the mountains. There are four extra bedrooms. One will be for your parents when they come to visit. The others are for our kids, assuming we have kids."

"That's a good assumption," Emily interrupted.

"Right, and one bedroom is for your brother Murphy if you ever want to bring him here to live with us."

Emily put her arms around his neck and hugged him tightly. "You're such a wonderful man. Thank you for that, Case. Murph is doing okay in Middlebury but just knowing I have the option to bring him here with me means the world to me, thank you. Now, I want to see Grandpa and Lupita before you take me to bed."

They slept late the next morning then showered together and got ready to go into Boulder to the builder's office to make paint color selections. Case insisted that Emily make the decisions about which room would be painted this color or that color. They laid out a set of plans for her and she wrote the selections in each individual room. Then they went to the lighting fixture supplier to pick out light fixtures for each room. It was a time consuming and laborious task but a necessary one. If they did not make the selections, then a representative from the builder would make the decision for them. They might not like the selections and replacing them would cost double.

"I never realized there was so much involved in building a house," Emily said.

"Neither did I," Case replied. "That's why I wanted you to do it."

"Oh, thanks a lot, tough guy."

With the house business taken care of, they went back to the ranch and Lupita made dinner for them.

James made a roaring fire in the fireplace and they all sat around talking and drinking coffee until very late. Lupita made Emily a cup of hot tea before she went upstairs to bed.

"Don't you think it's time you two kids got married?" James said.

Case and Emily looked at each other and smiled.

"Does it offend you that we sleep together out of wedlock, Grandpa?" Emily asked him.

"No, not really," James replied. "Oh, there was a time when it would have but I guess I've evolved. In my mind, you are already married. I mean, a blind man could see you love each other. I was just wondering."

She explained to him her reason for holding off on their getting married until after she had finished her obligation to her job and had moved back to Colorado. James seemed to accept that with some reticence.

"I wanted to give Case time to be absolutely sure that this was what he wanted. I hope you understand."

"Well, he's building you a house out there in the east meadow," James said. "I'm pretty sure he's sure."

They all laughed at that.

"I'd say you're right. But I made a commitment and I really want to stick to it. Case understands, and he knows I love him. And I know he loves me."

"I know he does, missy, and I do too, so you do what you know is right, and we'll all be waiting for you when you're ready to come home. It can't be soon enough for me because you remind me so much of Case's grand-mother, it's almost like she's still here when you're around. She was strong-willed and principled like you are. If she ever gave you her word, a herd of horses couldn't stop her from making good on it."

Emily went over and hugged him. "I know where Case gets his strength from, Grandpa. I love you too. I will be back as soon as I've kept my word. I promise you that."

Case drove her to DIA and walked her as far as he could into the concourse without going through security. He kissed her goodbye and watched her as she walked away. He didn't stop watching her until she got to her gate, turned, and waved to him, and then disappeared from his sight. Then he went back to his truck.

She caught the shuttle at the Burlington Airport and it dropped her off at her apartment. She called Case to let him know she had made it back okay.

The following February, on a Monday morning, when she got to her office, Emily had an email from Doc-tor Shelby, informing her of a meeting that would require her attendance on the twenty-fifth of the month. She told Sarah about it and expressed some curiosity about why she had been notified to be at the meeting.

"Maybe you're getting a promotion, Emily," Sarah said.

"To what, and for what?"

"Are you kidding? You're the best there is at this

kind of work. Everybody says so. And not just Doctor Shelby, who has a hard-on for you, but Mrs. Winters says so too. I wouldn't be the least bit surprised if this is a promotion of some kind for you."

"Well, a promotion won't get me back to Colorado any sooner. That's what I really need."

"Are you sorry now that you agreed to work for them four years?"

"No, not really. I get bummed out sometimes. When I was back there this past Christmas, Case showed me the house. It wasn't finished but the framework was all done and the walls were finished. It looked like a real house, just without the paint and cabinets and drapes and furniture and stuff. I'm still looking at two more years here. I get so lonely sometimes."

"Why don't you just quit and go home, Emily? They can't make you stay, even with a signed contract. Nobody would blame you if you just resigned."

"I can't do that, Sarah. It's not about the job, it about who I am. I gave my word. If I quit before I completed my commitment, I wouldn't respect myself and, more importantly, Case would not respect me. He would not go back on his word and I won't either. I could never do that."

"Well, I never will either because of you."

"Thank you, Sarah. I still wonder what that meeting is about."

"There's some big doings going on around here,"

Agnes, the billing secretary, told Emily.

"Really, what's going on?"

"Big shots coming in for a meeting, that's all I know."

"There's a meeting on Thursday. I'll let you know what happens unless they swear me to secrecy. It may be one of those clandestine things where, if I tell you anything, I have to kill you afterward."

"Oh, you're just teasing me, Emily," Agnes said dismissively.

She was curious, however, about the meeting and why Doctor Shelby asked her to be there. She wouldn't dwell on it, though. There were more important things going on in her life right now than that meeting. There was a man in Colorado building her a home in a high mountain meadow.

CHAPTER 11

Going Home

A round the twelfth of the previous month, Emily had realized that she was late for her period. She wasn't all that concerned and just wrote it off to the stress of having to leave Case again and the flight back after being so happy at the ranch. But when, on the twenty-first, she had still not gotten her monthly, she bought a pregnancy test at the drug store and took it. It came up negative.

In February, she missed her next period and then she became concerned for real. She purchased another pregnancy test and this time it showed positive. "Oh crap, what am I going to do now?" she said to herself.

She looked up the number for an OBGYN and made

an appointment, informed the office that she needed to take the morning off, and went to the clinic of a Doctor Nelson.

They did her bloodwork, and a urine test, and ran some other tests and then directed her to wait in one of the examination rooms for a doctor to see her. Before too long the doctor, accompanied by a nurse, knocked on the door and entered.

"Hello, miss," he said. "I'm Doctor Nelson, how have you been feeling?"

"I've been feeling okay but I've missed two periods, and I took two pregnancy tests. The first one was negative but the second one showed positive," she told him."

"Are you on any kind of birth control?"

"I've been on the pill so I don't know what could have happened."

"Have you been under any undue stress lately?"

"Oh, gosh, yes. Being away from my new home and my parents too. Being alone here is enough."

He looked at his notepad for her name. "Are you married, Miss Quarters?"

"No, I'm engaged to be married."

"I see," he said. "Well, you may want to think about scheduling the wedding pretty soon."

"Are you telling me I'm pregnant for certain?" Emily said, more or less resigned to that fact already.

"I am, miss. You are indeed pregnant, about two months along. Do you live with your fiancé?"

"No, he lives in Colorado." He looked at her quizzically and she gave him a brief explanation of her situation and relationship with Case.

"You'll have to make a decision on whether or not you want to tell him about the baby and if you want to keep it or not."

"We'll keep the baby, of course," Emily said, emphatically.

"I just have to tell you that there are other options for a young lady in your situation."

"No, Doctor, there are not. We'll keep the baby."

"Okay, then," he said. "I'll give you a list of pediatricians in the Burlington area. I recommend you start seeing one right away."

"Thank you, Doctor, I will."

That hit her like a ton of bricks. Emily didn't know whether to jump for joy or start crying. She'd have to tell Case right away but she thought she would probably wait until after Doctor Shelby's meeting. She didn't want to have to deal with two traumas at the same time.

She told Sarah, her only trusted confidant at the facility. Sarah hugged her and congratulated her. "Are you happy about it?" Sarah asked her.

"I am but it's really a shock. I don't know how this is going to affect my employment."

"You'll take a leave of absence, of course. We have other people here who can fill in for you. Don't worry, that's my main advice, don't worry."

"I'm trying not to, but it's hard," Emily replied.

There were many rumors going around about the coming meeting of the administrators of the Burlington Group. Some speculated that Doctor Shelby might be promoted to a higher position in the corporate structure while others suggested that he might get the ax. It seemed that a company, any company, whether its product be healing or making widgets, was no less open to employee gossip and rumormongering than any other company.

Agnes, who had been at The Colchester longer than anyone, claimed they were expanding and the meeting was like a brain-trust, absorbing information and assessing talent for new facilities.

No one paid much attention to the older woman due to her proclivity to expound on any and every subject that arose at the facility.

Thursday came and Emily gathered her notepad and several pens, in case one quit working, and made her way to the conference room. She was the first one there except for Justin, the custodian, who was making coffee and setting out some snacks.

"Oh, I'm sorry," she said. "They told me two o'clock."

"They're always late for these things, miss," the man said. "They'll be along directly. Would you like a cup of coffee?"

"Yes, that sounds nice." She started walking toward the coffee bar.

"Have a seat, miss, I'll bring it to you," Justin said. "You're Miss Quarters, right?"

She nodded. "Call me Emily, and you're Justin?"

"Yes, ma'am, cream and sugar?"

"Just cream, Justin, thank you."

He brought the cup of coffee and sat it down in front of her along with a small silver creamer. "It's actually just milk but people always say cream."

"Milk is fine, Justin." She smiled at him and he smiled back.

"These other guys are gonna have to get their own because they won't let me stay here during the meeting. It's a top-secret thing, I guess," he said, chuckling.

Emily nodded and smiled, raising her coffee cup in a quasi-toast.

Soon the others were filing into the room. Doctor Shelby sat at the head of the table, flanked by two gentlemen in suits and Mrs. Winters. In all, there were five men and two women in addition to Shelby and Emily. Emily quickly wrote down the names of each individual at the table, although she doubted she would be able to remember any of them once she had left the meeting.

One of the men, a Mister Barton, delivered a powerpoint presentation on the history of The Burlington Group and all its associated partners and facilities around the country. They apparently had long-standing relations with several colleges and universities in the US, the most prominent being the Universities of Colorado and Georgia, and they were working on signing contracts for programs with several other institutions of higher learning, as this meeting was unfolding.

A film was shown that profiled several of the more prominent people in the organization. After about an hour and a half, they took a bathroom break. Justin brought in fresh coffee and some more snacks.

The last order of business was the planned programs for expansion and establishment of facilities in other states, specifically in states where they had working programs with colleges and universities. Emily was growing weary of the corporate humdrum and was glad she would never move into the upper echelon of any organization.

A man named Darren Lewis got up, went to the podium, and began to explain that plans were already under way for opening another facility which he would manage. The facility would be a school but would have no hospital. Mister Lewis's particular expertise was in school administration. "The new facility will open in about a month and will be located in Thornton, Colorado, to be close to our associate school, the University of Colorado."

Emily suddenly became interested in the meeting. "Oh, my God," she said quietly to herself. "This could be a dream come true."

Lewis continued speaking. "Doctor Shelby and Mrs. Winters both have recommended that Emily Quarters be transferred to the Thornton facility to serve as assistant school administrator, that is, if she would be willing to relocate."

"Yes, yes" Emily shouted emphatically. "I can leave tomorrow."

Shelby laughed and Lewis looked bewildered. "Don't look so confused, Darren," Shelby said. "Emily went to school at CU and her home and future family are now in Colorado. She was planning to go back there when she fulfilled her commitment to The Colchester. My guess is she will be most happy to relocate."

Emily's eyes filled with tears and her head was nodding up and down, telling Shelby yes to his speculation about her willingness to relocate.

Whether Agnes was psychic or had a hot-line to someone higher up in the company, no one would ever know, but on this one occasion she had been spot on.

"Sarah, you won't believe this. They are transferring me to Thornton, Colorado, to a company school there," Emily told her confidant later. "It's the answer to my prayers."

Sarah hugged her lovingly. "I'll miss you, Emily, but I'm so happy for you. Have you called Case yet?"

"I tried but he didn't answer his phone. I have to try again."

Emily went by the main office where Agnes was bragging about her precognition abilities regarding the company's plans to expand. Some of the women were grilling her on how she knew but Agnes was being coy.

Gayle suggested that she was sleeping with Doctor Shelby and they all got a laugh out of that.

Agnes nixed that theory when she said, "Shelby is so in love with Emily Quarters, he won't even look at another woman."

Most of the women were shocked to hear her say that. It was not a commonly known fact.

Astounded, Emily stared at Agnes. Although Sarah had pretty much said the same thing, Emily had not thought anyone else would even notice such a thing.

"Don't look at me like you didn't know, missy," Agnes said.

"Doctor Shelby has never been anything but totally professional around me, Agnes," Emily said. "And I resent your insulting his integrity."

"I wasn't insulting his integrity, Emily. I was just saying he's in love with you."

"Well, you shouldn't start rumors or pass them on. That sort of thing can hurt people."

"I'm sorry," Agnes said, sensing Emily's seriousness on the subject. "I didn't mean any harm. Let's just drop it."

At that moment, Marie walked into the office. She was coming back from a late lunch and spotted Emily standing there in the office with the other women. "Emily, didn't you say your guy drives a red pickup truck?"

"Yes, he does. Why?"

"Well, there's a guy with 'panty-dropping eyes' sitting in a red pickup with Colorado plates in our parking lot, right out front."

"Are you serious?"

"Go look for yourself," Marie said.

Emily stepped out of the main doors onto the landing and looked toward the parking lot. Sure enough, there was Case sitting in his truck, all right, but the bed of the truck was loaded up with stuff and covered with a canvas tarp. And it looked like the extended cab was packed with clothes and other things. She began walking toward the truck. When he spotted her, he got out and started walking toward her.

"I can't believe my eyes," she said. "What are you doing here, darling? I mean, don't get me wrong, I'm thrilled to see you, but what are you doing here?"

"I realized about a week ago that I was not going to be able live without you for another two years, baby, so I decided to come here and get us an apartment and live with you until we can go back home."

"But what about the house?"

"Grandpa is going to oversee the work on the house, don't worry about it. All you have to do is finish your work here, and I'll do the dishes."

She put her arms around his neck and hugged him tightly. "You're absolutely unbelievable. I can't believe you'd leave Colorado for me."

"I did it for me too, honey, I've been a wreck of a man since you left. I can't sleep, I can't eat, I can't think straight. Grandpa pretty much threatened to shoot me if I didn't get out of town and go to where you are."

Suddenly Emily put her hands up to both sides of her head and started laughing. The more she laughed, the harder she laughed.

Case looked at her like she'd lost her mind. "What is it? Let me in on the joke so I can laugh too."

Finally, she got control of herself and managed to speak without laughing. "I've been trying to call you all afternoon but you didn't answer your phone."

"I had it turned off so I wouldn't have to answer your calls. I wanted to surprise you."

"Well, it's a day for surprises, Case. You're not going to believe this. I have two surprises for you."

"Believe what, what's going on?"

"I was just informed today that the company is putting in a facility in Thornton, and they want me to transfer there in less than a month."

"Are you serious?" Case said, in disbelief.

"Yes, it's true. It's like a dream come true."

"It certainly is, baby. I've been praying something like this would happen. I finally gave up and packed my stuff and came here to be with you. Oh, what was the other surprise?"

"Before too long there is going to be someone around calling you Daddy."

"You're pregnant?" he yelled so loudly that some people in the parking lot turned to look.

"I am, two months, so we better get back to Colorado. I have to make an honest man out of you."

He fell on the ground flat on his back and lay there for quite some time, attracting the attention of numerous people coming and going in and out of the facility.

"Wow, take a good look at me, Em, you're looking at a man who found a diamond in a goat's ass. This is too much for me all in one day. If I start bawling, you better not tell my Grandpa."

"I won't pretend I understand your esoteric euphemisms but I assume that remark was intended to register your delight in the news you just received, and if you do start bawling, I will tell Lupita."

Finally, he stood up. "I guess I could live with that. I don't know how it happened, with you on the pill, but I'm glad it did. I'm happy, Emily. I'm really happy about it. So, what's next, I guess we won't need that apartment now, will we? And I don't know what that word is you used."

"I guess we won't. We can stay in my place. I'll be finished up here and ready to leave in about a month. I'd like for you to stay with me until then. Esoteric is a term for things that only cowboys and outlaws understand."

"Oh, okay, I'll try to remember that. Here's what I'll do. I'll take my stuff back home and fly back. When you're ready to move, we'll get a rental truck and haul your stuff and your car back to the ranch. I can stay with you in your apartment until you're finished up here. If there's time left on your lease, we'll just pay it off. That will give you time to see your parents and we'll get married when we get back home."

"I like the plan," Emily said.

When Case pulled back into the ranch with all his stuff still in his truck, the look on his grandfather's face was priceless. "Relax, Grandpa, I didn't foul things up. I have good news. Let's go in the house and I'll tell you." He told him about Emily's transfer and how he was going back to bring her back to Colorado. "Oh, and you're going to be a great-grandfather."

"I thought I already was a great grandfather."

"No, I mean Emily is going to have a baby. You're going to be a great-grandfather."

"No shit, that's a wonderful thing, Case. I'm glad to hear it. So, you'd better get that house finished then. You don't want your wife and baby living in the barn, do you?"

"Didn't Mom and Dad live in the barn?"

"Well, yeah, but that was a long time ago."

"But the barn apartment was the same size, wasn't it?" Case said.

"Oh, all right, I just thought you wanted to get the house ready for her right away."

"I do, Grandpa, but it's more important that I go back to Vermont and bring her home."

"I guess you're right," James said.

Emily managed to get The Colchester to release her

two weeks early, due to her condition. And very soon they were loaded up and headed across New York on their way back to the rest of their lives. "It'll be a couple of months before the house is finished so we'll have to live in the barn apartment until then," Case said.

"A minor problem," she replied. "Your apartment is quite comfortable. I enjoyed every night I stayed there. I don't have to be on the job for two weeks so I want to relax for a while."

"Yeah, me too. I feel like I just made this trip."

"You're full of surprises, Case MacNicol. I have to admit, I never expected to see you sitting out there in the parking lot. I never thought you would leave your ranch and come to live in Vermont, even if it was only for two years."

"I came to be with you. It didn't matter where it was."

"Yeah, I remember you said that, even in Texas."

"Yep," he said, "even in Texas."

They spent two nights in motels, and Emily insisted on paying for it. "They gave me five-thousand dollars for relocation expenses. I told you that when I paid for the rental truck."

"I know, I just figured you could put that to your own use. I don't mind paying for things. I got my dad's inheritance when I turned twenty-five. We're rich, Em, filthy rich."

"Well, don't let it go to your head, cowboy," she said.

"I won't. I was already rich. You are the only thing I let go to my head. You are the only thing I need, you and the baby, I mean. The money doesn't hurt, of course."

"I don't want to live off of your money, Case. I want to keep working. I really love what I do. I like making a good paycheck, but I think I would keep doing it if I only made minimum wage."

"I wouldn't," he said. "The enjoyment of a job varies inversely to the amount of money a person makes doing it. No job is so rewarding that a man will do it for nothing, or for very little pay. It's just human nature, darlin'. That's just the way it is. I hope you never have to find that out the hard way, but take my word for it."

The first order of business was the wedding.

"You do still want to marry me, don't you?" she asked him.

"I'm willing to give it a try," he said.

"Oh, so now you're trying to wiggle out of it, when the time comes to tie the knot."

"Baby, you couldn't get rid of me with a court order," he said.

"I don't want to get rid of you, tough guy. Marry me or I'll cut your balls off."

"Well, I sure wouldn't marry you if you did that."

The wedding was going to be held at the ranch. James knew a back-sliding preacher from a local Baptist church and he agreed to perform the ceremony. Emily asked James MacNicol to give her away since her father could not be there. She had her hair done up on top of her head with ringlets hanging down on both sides. She bought a beige "Edwardian" style dress to hide her slightly protruding baby bump.

One of the invited male guests was so enamored with her that he asked her to run off with him, claiming she was the prettiest woman he'd ever laid eyes on.

Case asked Martin to be his best man. "You're the only friend I have," he told him.

"Do you ever wonder why you don't have any male friends, Case?" Martin asked him.

"No, I know why."

"Because they're afraid to bring their wives and girlfriends around you, right?"

"That's all I can figure. But I've changed now. The truth is I just don't know any guys that I care to hang out with. I wish you would bring your wife to Boulder. I'd like to have another couple for me and Emily to visit with and go places together sometimes. I might turn into a social animal."

"I'm working on it, Case, believe me, I'm working on it. And I'd consider it an honor to be your best man. I'd be happy to do it."

"Thanks, Martin, I appreciate it."

Emily called Mara and asked her to be her bridesmaid. Mara was the only person left from school that she knew in Colorado so it seemed appropriate, since she and Case had gotten together at her wedding. At Case's encouragement, Martin brought some of the folks from the BBG along with him. He did not invite Angie, figuring that her presence would not be helpful to the proceedings. Case hired his catering crew to prepare food for the affair. Jeremy and Mara showed up on time and brought some things for the house.

James directed the setting up of the chairs and podium in front of the new house, even though it was still unfinished.

"I want to get as far away as possible from the alpaca shit, Preacher," James explained.

"Well, I certainly do appreciate that, James," the preacher replied.

By the time they were ready to start the proceedings, the preacher was three sheets in the wind, but he arose to accept the challenge. "Brethren, and Sisteren" he began, and started laughing.

Case and Emily just looked at each other and waited for him to stop.

"We are gathered here today in the sight of God, friends, and neighbors, and at least a hundred alpacas, to witness the joining of Casey James MacNicol and Emily Ann Quarters in holy matrimony." Despite his slightly inebriated condition, he managed to administer the nuptials with appropriate Christian reverence.

"Do you Casey take this woman to be your wife?"

"I do," Case said.

"And do you Emily take this guy here to be your husband?"

"I do," she said, chuckling and rolling her eyes.

"If you ain't gonna kiss her, I will," the preacher said.

"Hold on there, Padre," Case said. "I'll do the kissing here."

He took Emily in his arms, kissed her, and dipped her backward then pulled her back upright, without ever taking his lips off of hers.

"I now pronounce you man and wife. May God bless this marriage and the children that are produced from it. May their love last as long as the mountains that surround us and be as beautiful as the blue Colorado skies above our heads, Amen."

"That's my kind of preacher, Grandpa," Case told James.

"He's not a bad guy when he's sober, but he's so rarely sober," James responded.

Somebody, who was going through the beer coolers, yelled at Case. "Hey, Case, is Coors the only kind of beer you have here?"

"No, man," Case yelled back. "It's just Coors on that side, look in those coolers over there on the other side, there's some Coors Light."

By ten o'clock that night, everyone had left but Jeremy and Mara. They stayed until eleven because Jeremy wanted to talk about his two alpacas. He and Case talked between themselves and seemed to get on quite well. Mara intimated that she was hoping that they might remain friends with her and Case. Emily didn't give her much encouragement, knowing that Case would not fit in, with the crowd they travelled in, in Evergreen. She perceived that it was more likely that Mara was wanting to manufacture a friendship between them so she could stay in close proximity to Case.

Once everyone had left the ranch, and Grandpa and Lupita had gone into the house, Case carried Emily through the door of the apartment, and laid her down on the bed.

"This all started with a handshake, Emily, and now here we are. I started thinking about this day the first time we danced. I promise you, Emily, I'll never raise my hand or my voice to you and I'll love you every day till I die."

"And I'll be everything you hoped I would be. You're all I'll ever want or need, Case. You are the love of my life and I'll love you too until we both die. Now shut up, take off your clothes, and turn off the light."

CHAPTER 12

Amy

E mily got the address of the new school facility in Thornton, and Case drove the route with her so she'd know the way. Even with morning traffic, it was no more than twenty-five minutes or so. She'd take 119 to Highway 36, the Denver-Boulder Turnpike to 287, and into Thornton. Darren Lewis had been onsite a month, interviewing staff members and teacher assistants to help Emily. The Thornton school was actually bigger and much nicer than The Colchester. Emily found it a quite comfortable working environment. Her only disappointment was that she could not see the mountains from the building. In fact, it was almost impossible to see them from anywhere in the town, because it was mostly flat, and buildings on both sides of the streets obscured the view, pretty much wherever she happened to be.

She had several classes and five teachers to oversee. Her job mostly consisted of advanced training. The teachers had the same educational qualifications as did Emily, but it was her experience and that special something about her that she brought to the table that placed her in a totally different level than the others. She was now doing primarily administrative work and began to miss working with the children.

That didn't last long because the first crisis of her tenure came in her second week on the job. Emily heard yelling from one of the classrooms and went to see what was causing the ruckus. An eight-year-old boy named Allen was yelling at Jo Carlyle, a teacher with a stocky frame and short, close-cropped hair. Emily had heard the other teachers suggest that Jo was of questionable gender association in that they were not sure if Jo was comfortable with her current gender identity. Jo had, however, a very good record of experience in dealing with autistic children. Her academics were admirable, and she'd never had a complaint. Nevertheless, as Emily entered the room Allen was reading Jo the riot act, so to speak. Emily quickly tried to calm the boy down.

"Tell me what's wrong, Allen," she said, but he kept ranting.

"Miss Jo is mean to me. Miss Jo won't let me go play outside."

"He wouldn't do his math lesson, Emily, and the punishment for that is loss of recess for one day."

"Miss Jo won't let me go play outside," Allen continued.

"Okay, stop a minute, Allen," Emily said to him. "Now you do know that you have to do your math, don't you?"

He nodded his head up and down.

"And you do know that if you don't do your math, you have to get some punishment for it, don't you?"

Again, he nodded.

"Okay then, why don't you tell me two punishments that you think would be fair for you to have to get if you don't do your lessons?"

He appeared to be thinking it over. "I think if I don't do my lessons Miss Jo tells me to do, I should not get to read the liberry books or play the video games for an hour."

"Then if Miss Jo thinks that's fair, one of those punishments will be your punishment the next time you won't do your lesson. But Miss Jo gets to pick which one, okay?"

He thought for a moment and then nodded again.

"Good, then we have a deal if Miss Jo is okay with it."

Jo gave them a thumbs up for acceptance.

"I see she is but now you still have to finish your math today, Allen. Okay?"

"Okay," he said and went back to his table.

"All right, thanks, Emily, that was pretty slick," Jo said.

"Different strokes for different folks, Jo. They are all different. Some tactics work on this one but not that one and vice versa. You have to figure out which tactic will work with which child. That thing I just did with Allen worked with several kids at the facility in Vermont but one smart guy suggested I force him to eat ice cream as a punishment. I didn't fall for it."

"Neither would I," Jo said, laughing.

One morning, Darren Lewis asked Emily to come into his office. "I have some bad news, Emily," he said. The inflection in his voice gave her a chill.

"What's wrong, Darren?" she asked, very apprehensive.

"I'm afraid that Jason Shelby has had a heart attack and is not expected to live. He's in intensive care now, in UVM Medical Center. I just thought you should know."

"I appreciate it, Darren. I'd like to go see him if I can take off a couple of days."

"Of course, you can, Emily. I only hope you can get there before it's too late."

Case looked confused when Emily drove through the gate. "What's up, baby, are you okay?"

"No, not really, Case. Doctor Shelby had a heart attack. He may die before I can get there, but I need to go see him before it's too late if I can."

"I'll go call and get us the tickets. I'd like to go with you, Emily, unless you want to go alone."

"No, I want you to go with me."

"Because of your condition, I mean," he said.

"I know, yes, I want you to come with me."

After they were in the air, she took his hand and squeezed it, gazing at him adoringly. "Thank you for coming with me, Case."

"It's my job, honey, to look out for you."

"There's something I have to tell you, nothing earth-shaking just something."

"Okay, shoot," he said

"Doctor Shelby, you know, came to my house, with Margaret Winters, when I was sixteen to examine Murphy and to more or less interview me about my work with my brother. He is pretty much totally responsible for my being able to come to Boulder and CU and you."

"I know, you've told me this before. I'll always be grateful to him for that."

"He is also rumored to be in love with me."

"Well, why wouldn't he be?" Case said, unfazed. "You're brilliant, you're beautiful, and you are totally dedicated to your job. He trusted you enough to finance four years of college on a promise that you would fulfill an obligation, and you did it. How could a man not fall in love with you?"

"Okay, I'm glad you're handling it so well, but that is not why I'm coming to see him."

"I didn't think it was, Emily. Like you said. The man gave you a chance to realize your dream. He gave you a chance to shine and you shined, or is it shone?"

"Both are correct, depending on the reference. He 'shined' his shoes because it has an object but he 'shone' which has no object."

"And you shone as bright as the stars."

"Thank you, and keep this in mind, he never once said a word to me about his feelings for me. I heard it from office personnel and, even then, it was just their perception."

They landed at the Burlington Airport, rented a car, and drove to the hospital, which was just down the street from The Colchester.

"I'm here to see Doctor Jason Shelby," Emily told the receiving nurse.

"What's your name, ma'am?"

"Emily MacNicol, I used to work for Doctor Shelby."

"I'll have to call his office for authorization," the nurse said. "Doctor Shelby has no immediate family in Vermont so they have put Agnes Cuddy in charge of approving visitation."

"I know Agnes," Emily said. "Tell her it's Emily Quarters. MacNicol is my married name."

After a moment, someone picked up on the other end of the line and the nurse gave her Emily's name. There was discernable excitement on the phone and Emily could imagine Agnes telling other women in the office that she was on the phone with Emily. Then the nurse looked up at Case and smiled. "Yes, Agnes, her husband is with her. No, I'm not going to tell you that, you'll have to look at him and judge for yourself." She was visibly embarrassed when she hung up the phone. "You can go in now. It's Room 134. Oh, and Agnes wants you to come by the office when you leave here."

The doctor was awake and seemingly aware when Emily and Case walked into the room. He brightened up when he saw Emily and put out his hand. She took it, noting that it felt very weak in hers, much weaker than she remembered when they had shaken hands in the past.

"This is quite an honor for me that you would come all the way from Colorado to see me, Emily. Thank you. I am happy to see you. And this is your rancher?" he said, looking at Case and extending his hand.

"I'm the culprit," Case replied. "Glad to meet you, sir."

"And I am equally happy to meet you, sir. I've heard great things about you."

"I could say the same about you, Doc."

"Well, we have both been blessed to have had this young lady in our lives. Emily is a very special person. She has done so much to enrich so many people's lives, we couldn't count them all."

"You can add me to that number because she saved mine," Case said.

Shelby chuckled, although it was a weak laugh. "And I can see by her attire that she's about to bring another one into the world. Are you hoping for a boy or a girl?"

"Emily wants a boy but my grandpa says I deserve to have a daughter so I'll have to worry about what kind of boy she takes up with."

"We really don't care which one it is, as long as he or she is healthy," Emily said.

"I'm happy for you, I'm sure he or she will be perfect."

"Thank you, Doctor," she replied.

The nurse entered the room and informed them that their visitation time was limited because of Shelby's weakening condition. Case told the doctor goodbye and walked out into the hall leaving Emily alone in the room with him.

"He's a fine man, Emily, I'm happy for you."

Thank you, Doctor. I'm so sorry for your misfortune. I'll pray for your fast recovery."

"I'll be okay, and call me Jason, for gosh sake. It really means a lot that you guys came to see me. I appreciate it more than you know."

She hugged him, told him goodbye and left the room.

They made an obligatory stop at The Colchester office and Agnes and the ladies there were surprisingly subdued and restrained. Case shook hands with each and every one of them as they eyed him up admiringly.

Agnes, displaying her unique sense of humor, looked askance at Case and turned to Emily. "I thought you said he was good looking, Emily."

Everyone laughed as Case stepped up to Agnes quickly. "I may not be good looking, Agnes, but I'm a really good dancer." He took her in his arms and hugged her, then he dipped her back, held her for a moment, and brought her back up, and stared into her eyes for a few seconds. Agnes looked like she was going to faint. She thoroughly enjoyed the attention.

He and Emily spent the night in a hotel and left the next morning to fly back home.

By the end of June, the house was finished and the utility company had tied in the permanent power. The individual trades had completed their work and gotten their final inspections. Case and Emily started moving in. The furniture was delivered and set up. Case decided to leave the barn apartment as it was to be used for a guest house when people came to visit or for out of town workers who sometimes came for a few days at a time when the ranch needed extra hands. Case and Emily spent most of their first night in their new home on the patio looking at the stars and the moon shining on the mountains.

It was none too soon, for Emily had taken to waddling around in maternity clothes, at work and on the ranch. Case was becoming concerned about her driving to and from work in her condition. He offered to start taking her and picking her up but she nixed that. "You are the most independent woman I have ever known, except maybe for Lupita," Case said. "Come on, Em, let me drive you in and pick you up."

"I'm okay, darling. Maybe when I get a bit further along."

James became like a doting father to Emily and he couldn't help expressing the same concern for her that Case had been pressing her about.

"You really ought to listen to your husband, honey. Summertime that turnpike gets as busy as a one-legged man in an ass-kicking contest." Then he just walked on by.

She started laughing at what he'd said and it suddenly registered on her. Case had been raised by his grandfather. Lupita had taken care of him when he was little boy but it was James MacNicol who constructed the man, Case MacNicol. He talked like his grandfather, acted like his grandfather, and thought like his grandfather. James MacNicol was a picture of Case in about forty years. And it wasn't all that bad a picture.

Emily was finally starting to understand the simple language the two of them spoke. She was the diamond he'd found in an imperfect and sullied world. What greater tribute could a man give a woman than that? A more educated and culture man might say it differently and with prettier words but no one could ever say it more sincerely. She was so blessed to be a member of the MacNicol clan.

One afternoon Lupita was helping Emily put away things in the kitchen of the new house and a Hispanic man made a delivery. He was a man Lupita knew and he asked about Emily.

"Who is the lady?" he asked in Spanish.

"The lady is my Casey's wife," Lupita replied, also in Spanish. "She is going to have a baby."

The man smiled at Emily and tipped his hat. Later, Emily asked Case about something that Lupita had said.

"Lupita said something like *una luz*. I couldn't understand it all but she was pointing at my stomach."

"*Para dar una luz?*"

"That's it. That's what she said,"

"That's a saying in the Spanish culture which, translated literally, means to give a light. A woman who is going to have a baby is going to 'give a light' or more specifically, she's going to bring a light into the world. It's a romantic concept, poetic, I suppose."

"It's beautiful." Emily said.

She relented and began allowing Case to drive her to work in the morning and pick her up in the afternoon, not because she felt as if she needed it but because *he* needed to do it. It was for his own peace of mind, and she accepted that.

She also agreed to get a sonogram to determine the gender of the baby. Until now, Emily had been content to wait and find out the old-fashioned way by waiting until the baby was born, but Case wanted to know. Case was the first to inform her of the baby's gender, in a language that only he understood.

The doctor pointed to a spot on the screen and mouthed the word to Case. "Girl."

Case looked at the image closely. "Grandpa wins," he said

"I don't know what that means, Case," Emily said.

"It's a girl," the doctor told her.

"It's a girl, Em, we're having a girl," Case reiterated.

"Are you okay with that, Case?"

"Yes, of course I am. A baby girl, she'll look just like you. We'll name her Emily, after you."

"No, I already have a name in mind," she said. "I want to name her Amy, after your grandmother."

"I think that's just fine. I love it and Grandpa will love it too. Thank you, baby."

In September, Amy Lupita MacNicol came into the world to the great delight of all those who knew her. Case took pictures of mother and daughter in the hospital bed and emailed them to Emily's parents. He then gave them a call to fill them in on how Emily and the baby were doing. Norman thanked him for being so considerate.

"She's your granddaughter, Norman. Of course, I was going to let you know," Case said. "You're welcome to come anytime for a visit to see her. I know Emily would love for you to come."

Norman said they would make every effort to make a visit in the near future.

"If they come, I will be surprised," Emily said.

"Really, why?"

"They just don't leave home very easily. I don't think they've ever been out of Vermont."

"Well, why don't we buy them plane tickets and bring them here for a few days to see the baby?"

"If they will come, that would be wonderful."

The Quarters family did come to see their granddaughter on her first birthday. Amy became confused when her daddy introduced her to her 'Grandpa' Norman, as she was accustomed, to having only one grandpa, and that was James MacNicol. But she eventually warmed up to the man and to Edna Quarters. Murphy was infatuated with the alpacas and chased after them. When Norman called him down for doing it, James said, "Let him go, Norman, he can't hurt them. They'll have more fun than Murphy does."

By the time their visit was over, the two families were much closer together, than they had been before. And the Quarters promised to come back in the future. They were proud of their daughter and at least as happy with their son-in-law as they were impressed with all he had done for her.

Like a typically reserved New Englander, Norman shook Case's hand as they were saying their goodbyes at the airport, and told him. "I'm really happy my daughter met you, Case. At first, I was a little skeptical of you because I didn't understand you, but you're a good man and you have a great family. I know that Emily and Amy are in good hands. Thank you."

"Thank you, Norman for Emily. She saved my life. And thanks for coming to visit. I look forward to the next time. We'll come to Vermont as soon as Amy is a little older."

A casual visitor to or passerby of Magnolia Road Ranch would usually see Lupita, and the two dogs, chasing after Amy MacNicol, trying to keep her out of the alpaca pen or the pond or just to find her hiding in the herd. She eventually grew too tall to hide among the little animals without being easily seen because her head was higher than their backs.

When Amy was three years-old, the family gathered for the official MacNicol clan picture. Case hired a professional photographer to come to the ranch with his crew to shoot his "masterpiece" for them. Case gave his plan to the photographer in intricate detail. Lupita, being the shortest, was in front with Amy who was sitting on Rudy, the red prize-winning 'paca. James and Case were in the rear with Emily standing between them.

Case's horse was behind him with his head looking over Case's left shoulder. Bogie and Bacall were lying down in front next to Rudy. Case had the photographer develop the picture in an old time black and white style. It hangs in the living room of the new house even to this day.

End of Story

About the Author

Jack Sprouse is from Dallas, Texas, although he now lives in Lewisville, a few miles north of Dallas. He studied American History at Texas Tech, in Lubbock, and his fields of greatest historical interest are the American Civil War and World War II. He served in the United States Navy as a crewmember on an ASW (anti-submarine-warfare) patrol aircraft. Writing fiction is his passion.

Sprouse just loves making stuff up (his mom used to punish him for doing that when he was a kid). He has written two books of historical fiction, *Adventures in Time ~ Book I: The American Civil War* and *Adventures in Time ~ Book II: The American West*, both Walter Mitty type stories in which he places himself back in time as a war correspondent following historical events and interviewing the major players in those events; two books of original poetry, *The Quiet Place* and *Dreams of a Forgotten Man,* both containing approximately fifty original poems on various subjects: life, love, friendship, relationships, war, conflict, tragedy; and several novels: *The House Wren*, a saga of a fictional Texas family; *On Neptune Wings*, a love story set in the 1960s against the backdrop of a US Navy Patrol Squadron; *Magnolia Road*, an improbable love story between a girl from Vermont and a rancher from Colorado; and *Clare*, about a twenty-four-year-old woman who faces life with quiet confidence and inner turmoil, experiencing love, hurt, uncertainty, sexual harassment in the workplace, and tragedy. He is currently working on several ideas for new books.